Robert Norman, William Borough

The New Attractiue

Containing a Short Discourse of the Magnes or Loadstone - and Amongst

Other his Vertues

Robert Norman, William Borough

The New Attractiue
Containing a Short Discourse of the Magnes or Loadstone - and Amongst Other his Vertues

ISBN/EAN: 9783337127596

Printed in Europe, USA, Canada, Australia, Japan

Cover: Foto ©Andreas Hilbeck / pixelio.de

The new Attractiue

Containing a Short Diſcourſe of the *Magnes* or Loadſtone: and amongſt other his vertues, of a new diſcouered ſecret and ſubtill propertie, concerning the declination of the *Needle*, touched therewith vnder the plaine of *the Horizon*.

Now firſt founde out by *Robert Norman* Hydrographer.

HEEREVNTO ARE ANNEXED CERtaine neceſſary rules for the Arte of Nauigation: by the ſame R. N.

Newly corrected and amended by M. W. B

Imprinted at London by E. Allde, for Hugh Aſtley. 1596

TO THE RIGHT WORSHIPFVLL, M. WILLIAM BOrough Esquire, Comptroller of her Maiesties Nauie: *Robert Norman* wisheth increase of worshippe, with perfect felicitie.

ARchimedes, after long search made to finde out the fraudulent myxture of King Hierons golden Crowne: could not by any meanes attaine the secrete thereof, till at length by chaunce as he was Bathing himself, he obserued that still as his body entred into the water, it forced the same to ryse and runne ouer the Vessell: wherupon the matter of the Crowne comming to hys remembrance, and applying the manner of the water to his present purpose, hee was foorthwith mooued with suche exceeding ioy, that hee leapt sodainlye out of the water, and forgetting him selfe to bee naked, came crying to the King his Maister, I haue founde, I haue founde: So I (right Worshipfull, although in other respectes & points of learning and knowledge, I will not presume to compare with *Archimedes*, who is many waies incomparable, nor with any other learned Mathematician, being my selfe an vnlearned Mathematician) by occasion of my profession, making sundry experimentes of the *Magnes* stone, founde at length amongst many other effectes, this strange and newe propertie of Declining of the Needle: which forgetting or rather neglecting mine owne nakednesse and want of furniture to set foorth the matter, I haue heere in simple sorte proposed and published to the viewe of the

 world.

world. Wherein I consider, though the occasions were diuers, our cases are not vnlike. *Pithagoras* lykewyse that greate Philosopher, for the singular ioy conceiued of the invention of that excellente Theoreme of Rectangle Triangles, made a solempne sacrafice, offering therein an Oxe vnto the Muses, as testifieth *Vitruuius* the author also of the former example. So that wee see these men and sundry others that are mentioned in authors, being caried and ouercome wyth the incredible delight conceiued of their owne deuices and inuentions, though they followe partly the peculiar contentation of their priuat fancies, yet they seme chiefly to respect either the glorie of God or the furtheraunce of some publike commoditie. Whose good example in this behalfe I will indeuour to followe, when to reach their rare giftes otherwyse, is rather to bee wished, then hoped for. And seeyng it hath pleased God to make mee the instrument to open thys Noble secret, that his name might be glorified, and the commoditie of my Country procured therby, I thought it my duty to aduenture my credite, and make my name the obiect of slaunderous and carping tongues, rather then suche a secrete shoulde be concealed, and the vse thereof vnknowen.

Howe beneficiall the Arte and exercise of Nauigation is to this Realme, there is no man so simple but sees, by meanes whereof wee beeing secluded and diuided from the rest of the worlde, are notwithstanding as it were Citizens of the worlde, walking through euerie corner, and rounde about the same, and enioying all the commodities of the worlde. How necessary the perfecte knowledge of the Needle or compasse is, to the perfection of the Art of Nauigation, your selfe who haue long time verie industriously trauailed therein and thereby in it, and other Sea causes excell others, can best iudge. To attaine vnto thys perfection, and to frame, as it were, a Theorike, wyth *Hypotheses*, and rules for the saluing of the apparant irregularitie of the Variation (if it bee a thing possible or within the compasse of mans capacitie) it must doubtlesse bee done by due obseruation of this new declining propertie,

wyth

with the Variation caused by the Admirable efficacie of the *Magnes* stone. Wherefore to further the Noble studye of Nauigation and Hydrography, and to giue ocasion to industrious & skilful trauailers by sea and by land, to make diligēt obseruation of these effects in sundry places, wherby some generall conclusion may be inferred, I haue heere set downe whatsoeuer I coulde finde by exact tryall, and perfect experiments, & besides this new property, diuers other rare effectes that followe this Philosophicall stone. Wherein although I may seeme to haue discouered my nakednesse, and want of eloquence and orderly Methode to vtter my conceites withall, I trust the reader will either of his curtesie take all thinges for good that is well ment, or of his grauitie not regarding the wordes but the matter, dissemble my faultes, and accept of my paines. And whereas amongst diuers learned and expert men in the Mathematicall sciences, to whome I haue imparted thys secret, I haue first of all and chiefly from time to tyme shewed the manner of it to your Worshippe, which first gaue occasion that I fell into the consideration thereof, and through whose encouragement I entred into farther examination of the matter, which otherwise I had neglected: If my trauell heerein take such effecte, that others be benefited or pleasured thereby, I haue my desire, and they are to be thankfull vnto you for the same, for I must needs ascribe the occasion to your good counsaile. To you therefore as to the most worthy and best acquainted wyth the cause, I present the first sight of this my rude and simple draught, which I trust, according to your accustomed curtesie and friendly affection towardes me, you will take in as good parte, as it proceedes from a harty good will towards you, whom I pray God long to preserue with all increase of Worship to his good pleasure.

Your Worships most humble, Robert Norman.

To the Reader.

Many and diuers ancient Authors, Philosophers & others, haue written of the Magnes or Loadstone, as also of the substaunce, vertue and operation, and thereupon setting downe their opinions and iudgementes, haue lefte the same as infallible truthes for them that shall succeede. And as I may not, nor meane not heerin willingly to condemne the learned or ancient wryters, that haue with great dilligence laboured to discouer the secrets of Nature in sundrie things, with their operations & causes: yet I meane God willing, without derogating from them, or exalting my selfe, to set downe a late experimented truth found in this stone, contrarie to the opinions of all them that haue heeretofore written thereof. Wherein I meane not to vse barely, tedious coniectures or imaginations: but breeflye as I may, to passe it ouer, grounding my Arguments onely vpon experience, reason and demonstration, which are the grounds of Arts. And albeit, it may be said by the learned in the Mathematicalles, as hath beene already written by some, that th is no question or matter for a Mechanitian or Mariner meddle with, no more then is the finding of the longitud for that it must bee handled exquisitelye by Geometrica demonstration, and Arithmeticall Calculation: in whic Artes, they would haue all Mechanitians and Sea-men to be ignorant, or at leaste insufficientlie furnished to performe such a matter, alleaging against them the Latine

Prouerbe

Prouerbe of Apelles, *Ne sutor vltra crepidam*. But I doe verily thinke, that notwithstanding the learned in those Sciences, being in their studies amongst their bookes, can imagine greate matters, and sette downe their farre fetcht conceites, in faire showe, and with plawsible wordes wishing that all Mechanicians were such as for want of vtterance, should be forced to deliuer vnto them their knowledge and conceites, that they might flourishe vppon them, and applye them at their pleasures: yet there are in this land, diuers Mechanicians, that in their seuerall faculties and professions, haue the vse of those Artes at their fingers endes, and can apply them to their seuerell purposes, as effectually and more readily then those that would most condemne them. For albeit they haue not the vse of the Greeke and Latin tongues, to search the varietie of Authors in those Artes, yet they haue in English for Geometrie, Euclides Elementes, with absolute demonstrations: and for Arithmaticke, Records workes, both his first and seconde partes: and diuers others, both in English, and in other vulgar languages, that haue also written of them, which bookes are sufficient to the industrious Mechanician, to make him perfect and ready in those sciences, but especially to apply the same to the Art and faculty which he chiefly professeth. And therefore I woulde wish the learned to vse modestie in publishing their conceites, and not disdainfully to condemne men that will search out the secretes of their artes and professions, and publishe the same to the behoofe and vse of others, no more then they woulde that others shoulde iudge of them, for promising much and performing little or nothing at all. Aristotle saith, that euerie man is best to be beleeued in his owne professed Art and Science. Now (curteous reader) I am to request thee to accept of this my discourse, wherein I haue taken some paines (as the trauaile it selfe may testifie) and beene at some charge, for the more carefull and orderly handling of such matters as are necessarily incident to this presente treatise: All which I haue beene content to doe, that the worke (though it bee not big, yet effectuall) by the common vse thereof, may yeeld profit accordingly, to them specially that are of capacitie to comprehend this new reuealed secret. To conclude, the chiefest and onely marke whereat I lay leuell, was the benefiting of my Country-men, in whom I wish continuall increase of knowledge and cunning, as in all other commendable professions, so chiefely in those that are most necessarie and profitable. Thus bequeathing my trauails heerein to thy discreet construction and wishing thy furtherance in this most necessarie and profitable knowledge, I leaue thee to the direction of Gods holy Spirit.

Fare-well,

Robert Norman.

The

The Magnes or Loadſtones Challenge.

GIue place ye glittering ſparkes,
ye glimmering Diamonds bright,
Ye Rubies red, and Saphires braue,
wherein ye moſt delight.
In breefe yee ſtones enricht,
and burniſht all with gold,
Set foorth in Lapidaries ſhops,
for Iewels to be ſolde.
Giue place, giue place I ſay,
your beautie, gleame, and glee,
Is all the vertue for the which,
accepted ſo you bee.
Magnes, the Loadſtone I,
your painted ſheaths defie,
Without my helpe, in Indian ſeas
the beſt of you might lye.
I guide the Pilats courſe,
his helping hand I am,
The Mariner delights in me,
ſo doth the Marchant man.
My vertue lies vnknowen,
my ſecretes hidden are,
By me the Court and Common weale,
are pleaſured verie farre.
No ſhip could ſayle on ſeas,
her courſe to runne aright,
Nor compaſſe ſhew the ready way,
were Magnes not of might.

Bluſh

Blush then, and blemish all,
bequeath to mee thats due,
Your seates in golde, your price in plate,
which Iewellers doo renue.
Its I, its I alone,
whom you vsurpe vpon,
Magnes my name, the Loadstone cald,
the prince of stones alone.
If this you can denie,
then seeme to make reply,
And let the painefull sea-man iudge,
the which of vs dooth lye.

The Mariners iudgement.

THE Loadstone is the stone,
the onely stone alone,
Deseruing praise aboue the rest,
whose vertues are vnknowne.

The Marchants verdict.

THe Diamonds bright, the Saphirs braue,
are stones that beare the name,
But flatter not, and tell the troath,
Magnes deserues the fame.

The new Attractiue.

The first Chapter.

Of the Magnes or Loadstone, where they are found, and of their colours, weight, and vertue in drawing yron or steele: and of other properties of the same stone.

THE Magnes or Loadstone is found in diuers partes of the worlde, and most commonlie in Yron Mynes, and although it bee ponderous and weightie, yet it is not found to be of the Yron Ewre, neither conteineth in it any mettall of it selfe, but hath a certaine affinitie vnto yron or steele. It was called Magnes, because the first finder thereof was so named, who (as Plinie writeth) was an Herdsman in East India.

This stone (as writeth Cardinal Cusan) hath substance, vertue, and operation. His vertue is conserued & nourished of his substance: & of this vertue proceedeth diuers strange effects and operations, seruing to many good purposes, as specially in the Arte of Nauigation, without which there could haue beene no discoueries by sea, nor the partes of the world made knowne & frequented as now they are. And therefore the vertue of this stone of all others may bee accounted the most precious.

Of these are diuers sortes differing each from other, as well in goodnesse, as in colour, weight, and force, but not in propertie (although manie haue iudged the variation of the Needle, to bee according to the distance of the Mine where the stone was bred, to the place where hee is vsed:)

The

The first and best sort of these stones come out of the East India, from the coast of China, and Bengala, and is of the colour of yron or sanguine colour: these stones are verye massiue & weightie, & will drawe or lift vp the iust weight of it selfe in yron or steele (if the stone exceede not a pound weight.) And these are of the finest sort, and are sold commonly for their proper weight in siluer in the East India, where they growe, because the best & finest are verie rare to be found. For it is commonly a sole stone, lying by himselfe in the earth, and no shell or peece of another.

The best Loadstone.

There is another sort of a reddish colour found in Arabia and the red Sea, growing broad and flat, much like to a Tilestone or Slate: this is not so weyghtie as those of China, but it is verie neere as good, and the vertue continueth long on the Compasse or Needle that is touched with it.

Next the best.

There is likewise of these stones in Leuant, in the Ile of Elba, hard by a towne in the same Ilande called Porto Ferato, from whence our Mariners daylie bring of them, and are called there Calamita Preta, that is to say, The blacke Magnes, because there is another sort that is white and light, lyke vnto a peece of dry Fullers clay, and is called Calamita Blanca.

This Calamita Blanca is founde alwayes with the other, sticking fast in the out side thereof lyke claye. And this white is forbidden to be vsed in that Country, because euill women there, doo applye it to destroye conception, whereof this stone is a great enemie. Other thinges are noted of this white Calamita, for obtaining of wanton purposes, which I thinke not credible, and therefore will omit it. These blacke stones of Elba are mingled with white veynes, they are of no great force, nor their vertue of long continuance.

Also there are of these stones in high Almaine, that are full of holes like a hunnie combe, & lighter then the other, but yet very good, and these are of yron colour.

Another

Another sorte there is in Norwaie, in the yron Mines, as in Longsounde, and other places, their couleur is blacke, mixed or as it were interlarded with graie, these are of the smallest force of any that are found. The worst.

I haue séene also in the Mines of Carauaca in Spayne of a graie colour, but of no greate force: these are commonly brought by horse downe to Siuill and Caltis to bee sould, and oftentimes to Valentia, Alicante, and Lisbone.

All these stones are different one from another, as well in force as in colour and weight: yet all of one operation in the Néedle, shewing one pointe Attractiue, as I haue proued my selfe by thrée sundry sortes of them, which I haue: and all drawing yron to them. Yet the Philosopher Auerroes writeth that the Magnes draweth not yron vnto it, but the yron of his naturall inclination moueth to the Stone.

And though this position may séeme to carrye some trueth with it, by the bare veiw of the sight, when the yron is lighter then the Stone: yet contrariewyse you shall finde, that the Stone will moue to the yron, if the Stone bee good, and the yron of greater weight then the Stone (so that the weight of the Stone excéede not hys Attractiue strength.)

Neuerthelesse wee may not thereby take away the vitall or liuely spirite from the Stone, and attribute it vnto the yron: for in so doing we shoulde doe Nature greate wrong. For it is apparant, that the yron hath no Attractiue vertue, nor power of it selfe, vntill it haue receiued it of the stone. But yron hauing a certaine affinitie, or naturall quallitie agréeable to the stone, doth aptly and freely receiue his vertue, and as a subiecte, suffereth his vitall spirit of the stone to impresse, and rest quietly in his massiue and solide bodie, which when it hath receiued by touching the Stone, it is indued with the very same propertie and operations in all respectes (though not in so great force) as the stone it selfe. The vital and natural spirit & operation of the Load-stone.

For

For as the Stone hath power to shewe the Attractiue poinct, so hath the touched Yron. As the Stone hath two principall poinctes, so hath the Yron. And likewise, as the stone hath power to drawe yron to it, so will the Yron so touched, drawe another yron to it, and impart all these vertues to another yron in qualitie, though not in quantitie: and thus in all respectes it conteineth in it, the verie propertie of the stone.

Paracelsus writing of the augmenting of the Strength of the Magnes Stone saith, that if this Stone bee laide in the fire, untyll it bee almost redde hot, and then taken out and quenched in the Oyle of Crocus Martis, it will so augment and multiply his force, that it will pull a nayle out of a wall. But I suppose he meant not that the naile should be fast, for then it were a miraculous matter.

Others haue written, that in those partes, where the Magnes groweth in the Sea, it is of such force, that if anie Shippes that haue yron in them passe by, or ouer them, that they are presently either staied, or drawen downe to the bottome by reason of the yron. Not these onely, but many other fables haue béene written by those of auntyent time, that haue as it were set downe their owne imaginations for undoubted truthes, and this most of all in Geographie and Hidrographie, or Nauigation. Therefore I wishe experience to be the leader of Writers in those Artes, and reason their rule in setting it downe, that the followers be not led by them into errours, as oftentymes haue béene séene.

True it is, that God is mightie and maruellous in all his workes: yet hee doeth not allowe us to say more then truth of them. And truely, his power is as greatly shewed in the Magnes, as in any stone that hee hath created: and who so shall goe about curiouslie to séeke out the efficient cause of his properties, I suppose the longer hee séeketh, the more he shall maruaile, and yet neuer the néerer his purpose.

The vertue of the Stone is distributiue, as many other vertues are, much comparable vnto Muske, that hauing a swéet sauour or smell it selfe, imparteth the same to another thing, as to a paire of Gloues, and those Gloues giue out sauour, and perfume a whole chest of cloathes: Euen so the yron that hath receiued this vertue of the stone will extend, and giue the same to another, and that yron to another, and so to many.

And in this point the stone is maruellous, that notwithstanding you touch ten thousand yrons or nailes with him, euery one of them carrying away as much vertue as will lifte vp another his lyke (so they excéed not the weight of a sixe penny naile) yet the Stone it selfe will be nothing diminished of his strength, but continue of one force.

If I should say héere, that by the Attractiue strength of a small Magnes of two or thrée pounds weight, I could lift vppe, or cause to hange by the vertue thereof, a thousande pounde of yron at one instant, peraduenture you would bee doubtfull of the successe. Neuerthelesse by experience in all thinges, wherein consisteth truth and reason, of necessitie reason must yeild, when truth is present. And therefore because you shall not remaine doubtfull héerein, thus you may dooe it, and onely make proofe by two or thrée nailes, if you will: for the same successe that you haue in them, you shall haue in all the rest.

Take a common boord nayle, & touch the head of it with the North parte of the Magnes or Loadstone, then take the same nayle and beate it with a péece of woode lightly into some poste or timber vpwardes, so as the heade maye hange downe wardes, (but not with yron, because the yron will take away some parte of the vertue from the nayle:) this done, take another like naile, and touch the head thereof with the South parte of the Stone, and then if you put the head of it to the head of the first naile, it wil hang fast by it a whole yeere or more. And after this manner you may, if you wil take the paines, hang a hundred tun of iron with

the

the vertue of this little ſtone, and yet the ſtone nothing dyminiſhed of his force. But it is neceſſarie in proofe of this matter, that you haue a very good ſtone.

Irons to hang one by another by vertue of this ſtone.

Furthermore, concerning the other properties of thys ſtone, if you put it in a dry diſhe, and ſette it to ſwimme in a tub of Water, it will turne the diſh about, and the North parte of the ſtone, after many ſwaruinges to and fro, will reſt, and directly ſhewe the line of Variation, or imagined Attractiue point.

Alſo, if you hang this Stone by a thrid, that it may eaſilie mooue, it will ſhew the like effects as on the water. And if you haue two ſtones, putting the two South partes of them together, the one will fly and turne away from the other, and likewiſe of the North pointes.

A ſpecial note

And further yee ſhall note as a ſpeciall point, that the North point of the Stone touching a Néedle, or the wyers of a compaſſe, will make the ſame point touched to ſhewe the South: and contrariwiſe, beeing touched with the South point, wil make the ſame to ſhew the North, So as alwaies that part of the ſtone that anſwereth to the North of the Néedle, is properly the South part of the ſtone.

The ſecond Chapter.

Of the diuers opinions of thoſe that haue written of the Attractiue point, and where they haue imagined it to be.

31.

THE ſubtill properties and hid ſecretes of Nature in the Magnes, as alſo in dyuers other thinges, hath ſo troubled the wits of the ſearchers thereof, that alwayes when they came to the upſhot, wanting experience, and thereby reaſons finger to ſhew them a direct marke, they were conſtrained to ſéeke or imagine a marke, where in deede none at all was, and thus

ſhooting

shooting as it were in ẏ aire, euerie man where he thought best, they haue all shot wide, and none touched the marke. The marke I meane heere, is the point Attractiue, or rather, as shall bee saide heereafter more at large, the point Respectiue.

This point, auncientlŷ called the Attractiue point, hath beene by some imagined to be in the moouing spheres distant from the poles of the worlde: which opinion Martin Curtes in his Booke of Nauigation refuting, saith, that if it were so, then the same point beeing carried about the pole by their violent motion, woulde cause the Needle or Compasse touched with the vertue of the Stone, to varie dayly in euery place, according to the diurnall motion of the same sphere. But in confuting the erronious opinion, he hath (as it appeareth) fallen into as greate an error himselfe: imagining the poincte Attractiue to bee beyond the poles of the worlde, without all the mooueable heauens. Which point (saith he) hath power by Attraction to draw yron to it, that is touched with the Loadstone. This errour I referre to be discussed in the first Chapter.

Others haue taught this poinct to be in the earth, neere the North pole, imagining in that part to bee some great rocks of the Loadstone, & that by their Attraction the compasse or needle is caused to Respect or shew that part.

This opinion of all the rest is easiest to bee confuted by daily experience: for if the compasse or needle were drawn towardes the North parte by any Attraction of the Magnes stones in those partes imagined, why then should not the Compasse or Needle shewe the same effecte in moouing towardes the Iland of Elba in the Leuant seas, wher are great quantitie of these Stones? and yet Shippes sayling within a myle of this Iland, yea, and into Porto Feraro a Towne of the same Ile, within a quarter of a mile of a huge Rocke of these stones, the Compasse or Needle is not found any thing to be drawne or chaunged, nor the Attraction of this huge rocke to extend so farre as one quarter of a mile. And as I haue said by this, so may I say by diuers other places where the Loadstone are founde in Cliftes and Mines neere to the Sea side, as in Norwaie and other places.

Pedro de Media in his booke of Nauigation is of the opinion of Martin Curtes as touching the Attractiue point, but he doth not allowe of the variation of the compasse or needle, but saith, that if the compasse or needle shew not the pole, the fault is in placing the wiers on the flie, & not in any propertie it hath to vary.

These opinions by diuers, but the chiefest cause why they haue gone so farre wide from the Attractiue poynct, as I haue aboue said, was because they wanted reasons fingers to shewe them towardes the direct marke. By this reasons finger, I meane a certaine Declining propertie vnder the Horizon, lately founde in the Needle, which I will entreate off at large.

The third Chapter.

By what meanes the rare and straunge Declyning of the Needle, from the plaine of the Horizon was first found.

HAuing made many and diuers compasses, and vsing alwaies to finish and end them before I touched the Needle, I found continually that after I had touched the yrons with the Stone, that presently the North poynct thereof woulde bend or Declyne downwardes vnder the Horizon in some quantitie: insomuch that to the Flie of the Compasse, which before was made equall, I was still constrained to put some smal peece of waxe in the South parte thereof, to counterpoise this Declining, and to make it equall againe.

Which effecte hauing many times passed my handes

without

without any greate regarde thereunto, as ignorant of any such propertie in the Stone, and not before hauing hearde nor read of any such matter: I chaunced at length that there came to my handes an Instrument to bee made, with a Néedle of sixe inches long, which Needle after I had polished, cut of at Iust length, and made it to stand leuel vpon the pinne, so that nothing rested but onely the touching of it with the stone: when I hadde touched the same, presently the North part thereof Declined downe, in such sort, that beeing constrained to cut away some of that parte, to make it equall againe, in the end I cut it too short, and so spoiled the Néedle wherin I had taken so much paines.

Hereby beeing stroken into some cholar, I applyed my selfe to seeke further into this effecte, and making certaine learned and expert men, my friendes, acquainted in this matter, they aduise mée to frame some Instrument, to make some exact triall, how much the Néedle touched with the Stone woulde Decline, or what greatest Angle it would make with the plaine of the Horizon. Whereupon I made diligent proofes: the manner whereof is shewed in the Chapter following.

The fourth Chapter.

How to find the greatest Declining of the Needle vnder the Horizon.

Take a small Néedle of Steele wier of fiue or sixe inches long, the smaller and the finer mettall, the better and in the middle therof (crosse the same) by the best meanes you can, fixe as it were a small Axeltree of Iron or Brasse, of an inch long, or thereabout, and make the endes thereof verie sharpe whereupon the Néedle may hang leuell, and play at his pleasure.

Then prouide a round plaine Instrument like an Astrolobe, to be deuided exactly into 160. partes, whose diameter must be the length of the Needle, or thereabout, and the same instrument to bee placed vppon a foote of conuenient height, wyth a plumme lyne to sette it perpendicular.

Then in the Center of the same Instrument, place a peece of Glasse hollowed, and against the same Center vppon some place of Brasse that may bee fixed vpon the foote of the Instrument, fit another peece of Glasse, in such sorte that the sharpe endes of the Axeltree beeing borne in these two Glasses, the Needle may play freely at hys pleasure, according to the standing of the Instrument.

And the Needle must be so perfected, that it may hang vpon his Axeltree both endes leuell with the Horizon, or beeing turned, may stande and remaine at any place that it shall be sette: which being done, touch the saide Needle with the Magnes stone, and set the Instrument perpendicular by the plumme lyne, and turne the edge of the Instrument South and North, so as the Needle may stande duely according to the Variation of the place: which Variation the Needle of his owne propertie woulde shewe, were it not that hee is constrained to the contrary by the Axeltree.

Then shall you see the Declination of the North point of the touched Needle, which for this Cyty of London, I finde by exact obseruations to be about 71. degrees 50. mynutes. The forme of the Instrument heere described, with the manner of the declination, I haue heere placed that it may be the easier conceiued.

The

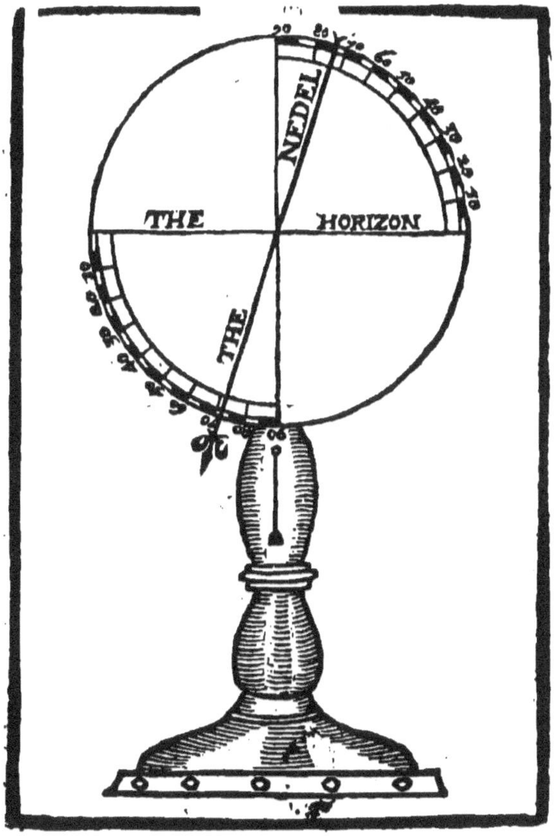

The fift Chapter.

That in the vertue of the Magnes or Loadstone, is no pondrous or weightie matter, to cause any such declining in the Needle.

BEcause the opinions of men are diuers, and the arguments of many against reason, peraduenture there are some will say, that I am deceiued euen in the grounde & chiefest point of this my purpose, alledging (as some haue already done without reason) that this Declining of the needle, is caused by some ponderous substance that it receiueth from the Stone, and not (as I take it) to procéede of the simple vertue, & secret influence thereof, because the stone it selfe wherein the vertue remaineth and is nourished, is weightie.

I iudge the learned will not allowe a Spirit to haue any corporall substance or weight, or that it may sensibly be felt: if any should, yet by two conclusions it is easily prooued, that the vertue of this stone containeth in it no weightie matter: and thus found.

Take thrée or foure small peeces of Iron or Stéele wier, and putting them in a fine gold Ballance, counterpoise them iustly with Leade: Then take them out and touch them well with the Stone, that they may receiue the vertue thereof: And after weigh them againe in the same ballance, with the same Lead, and you shall finde them to weigh no more, thẽ before they were touched, though euery one of them haue receiued vertue sufficient to lift vppe his fellowe.

Secondlie if the the North point of the Néedle do Decline by any ponderous or weightie matter, in the vertue receiued by touching the Stone, why then shoulde not the South poinct of the Néedle being touched with the contrary end of the Stone, haue the same declyning Southwardes, beeing all one Stone, and one vertue: Or why doth not this supposed heauier end, fall perpendicularly to the Center, as by reason it shoulde, and not couet a certaine scituation beside it, ballancing it selfe vp and downe, till it haue found the same? These argumentes may aunswere thys matter. For touch the Needle with what part of the Stone you liste, that end of the néedle that sheweth the North, wil alwaies decline.

The sixt Chapter.

A confutation of the common receiued opinion of the poinct Attractiue.

Séeing

SEing it is manifest that there is a Declining in the needle, and that the same is not caused by any ponderous waightie matter in the vertue receiued from the Stone: it may be demanded, by what meanes this declining or eleuating happneth & in which of the two pointes consisteth the action or cause thereof.

Peraduenture you will say (as other haue imagined) that it is in the South poinct of the Needle, eleuated by the Attractiue vertue of some poinct of the Heauen that way. Perchaunce you will yeeld it rather to be in the North poinct of the Needle, which by some Attractiue poinct in the Earth, or in the Heauens, beyond the Earth that way, is drawen downe and caused to declyne, and it Declining, of necessity the other South point opposite must needes be lifted vp.

Your reason towards the earth carrieth some probabylitie, but I proue that there be no Attractiue, or drawing propertie in neither of these two partes, then in the Attractiue point lost, and falsely called the poynt Attractiue, as shall be prooued. But because there is a certaine poinct, that the needle alwayes respecteth or sheweth, beeing voyde and without any Attractiue propertie, in my iudgement this poinct ought rather to bee called the poynt Respectiue.

And further if it may be proued, that there is no Attractiue or drawing propertie in that point, the power & action in that point condemned, then of necessitie the power and propertie, without any externall cause, remaineth onely in the Stone, and after in the needle beeing touched wyth it, hauing the same power & propertie in it, that the Stone hath in euerie respect.

Now to proue no Attractiue poinct neither beneath in the earth, nor Heauens Northwardes, nor aboue in the heauens Southwardes, you shall take a peece of Iron or

Stéele wier of two inches long or more, and thrust it into a peece of close Corke, as bigge as you thinke may sufficiently beare the wier on the water, so as the same Corke rest in the middle of the wier.

Then you shall take a déep Glasse, bole, cuppe, or other vessell, and fill it with faire water, setting it in some place where it may rest quiet and out of the winde. Thys done cut the Corke circumspectly by little and lyttle, untill the wier with the Corke bee so fitted, that it may remaine under the superficies of the water two or thrée inches, both endes of the wier lying leuill with the superficies of the water, wythout ascending or descending, lyke to the beame of a paire of ballance beeing equally poised at both endes.

Then take out of the same wier without mouing the Corke, and touch it with the Stone, the one end with the South of the Stone, and the other end with the North, and then sette it againe in the water, and you shall see it presently turne it selfe upon his owne Center, shewing the aforesaide Declining propertie, without descending to the bottome, as by reason it shoulde, if there were any Attraction downwardes, the lower part of the water being neerer that point, then the superficies thereof.

And as this may prooue no Attraction or drawing downwardes in like maner the Corke being so made, that it may sinke very slowly to the bottome, and then taken out and touched with the Stone, and put in againe downe to the bottome with your finger, if any Attractiue drawing were upwardes, it woulde ascend, and come up to the superficies of the water, beeing néerer to that point than the bottome. But I finde by diligent and exact triall, that it hath no such effecte: as in the figure following is demonstrated.

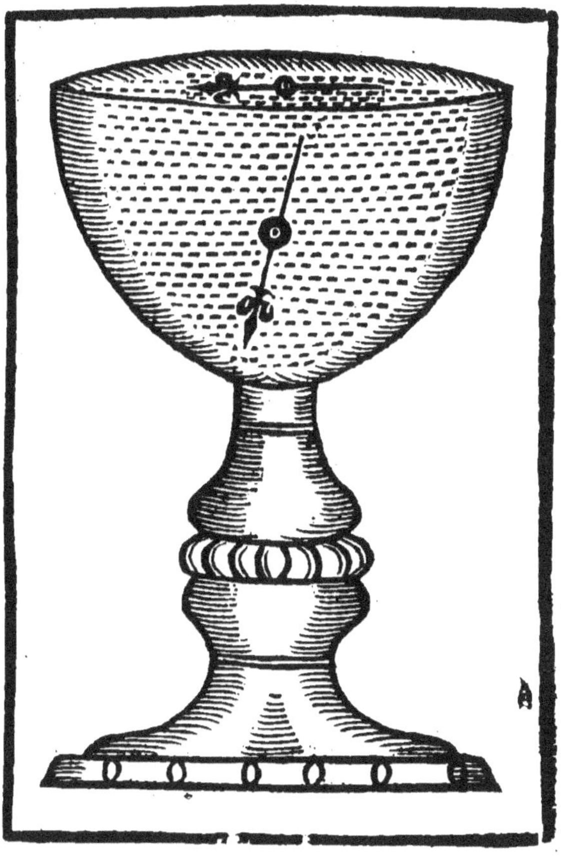

Againe, if you doe fit your wier with Corke, that after it is touched with the Stone, it will swim leuell in the superficies of the water, you shall see it turne to shew the true Variation, and leauing the same in the middle of the superficies of the water, so long as you list, you shall finde that it will not bee drawen from his place, neither to the

one

one side, nor the other, whereas if there were any suche Attractiue point as haue beene imagined, either in the earth by vertue of huge Rockes of the Magnes Stone neere the Pole, or otherwise in the heauen, or wheresoeuer, by what meanes soeuer, beeing but the twentith parte of the force that the Needle touched, hath to shewe to Respectiue point, it should of necessitie be drawen in time to some side.

So that vppon these experimentes I conclude, that the Attractiue poynt before imagined, is no where, nor no such thing: and therefore, as most proper, I will call the point whereunto the Needle inclineth by vertue of the Stone, The point Respectiue, and attribute the whole power of shewing that poynt to be in the Stone, and in the needle, by the vertue receiued of the Stone, which vertue must bee imagined to be turned, borne, and depending vpon his owne Center, as shall bee shewed in the next Chepter.

The seuenth Chapter.

Of the point Respectiue, where it may bee by greatest reason imagined.

This point Respectiue, is a certaine point, which the touched Needle doeth alwaies Respect or shew, and is found by the declyning of the neédle, to bee a pricke in some one part of a straight lyne, declyning in this place or Latitude of London vnder the Horizon 71. degrees, and 50. Minutes, as this figure following representeth.

This

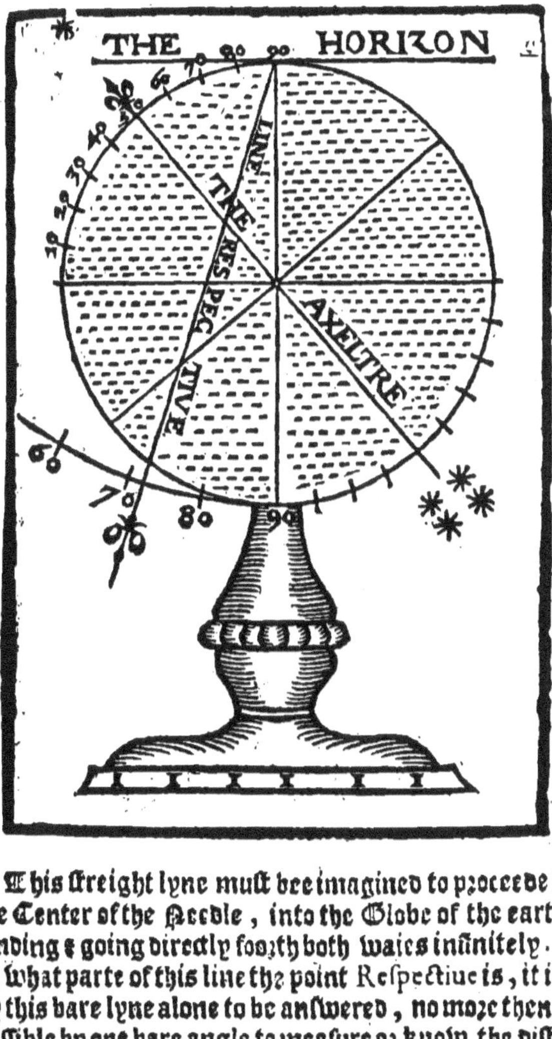

This streight lyne must bee imagined to procede from the Center of the Needle, into the Globe of the earth, extending & going directly foorth both waies infinitely. But in what parte of this line the point Respectiue is, it is not by this bare lyne alone to be answered, no more then it is possible by one bare angle to measure or know the distance of any place assigned.

And

And for the finding or certaine assigning of yͤ true place of this poinct Respectiue, we must leaue vntill the expert trauailer haue made certaine obseruation of thys Declyning of the Needle in other places. For seeing it is certaine that though in seuerall Horizons, the compasse hath seuerall Varations: yet in any one Horizon, the néedle Respecteth alwayes one onelie poinct without alteration, as by trauaile is truelie prooued. So I iudge, that in his Declinyng, it keepeth the like order and certaintie in euerye place.

And although the Needle of the Compasse, by reason of the weight of the heauie flie, cannot Decline, as hys propertie is, but falselie sheweth the poinct Respectiue alwaies in the Horizon, as most necessarie so to doo for the Nauigation: yet by the meanes and conclusions, whiche before I haue shewed, the diligent traueller hauing with him a good Magnes or Loadstone, may by exact obseruation finde the increasing or decreasing of this Declining of the needle, as his trauaile shall giue occasion.

For I am of this opinion, (and that by great reason) that this Declining of the Needle shall bee founde by trauell to be great or little, according as the distaunce of the poinct Respectiue, is from the place where the triall is made: whiche beeing diligentlie obserued in sundrie places, with the certaine Variation of the Needle from the Meridian, therby may bee demonstrated and found out the true place of this poinct Respectiue.

The eight Chapter.

Certeine proofes that the power and action is wholie and freelie in the stone, to shewe this poinct Respectiue: and in the Needle, by vertue & power receiued of the Stone: and not forced or constrayned by anie Attraction in heauen or earth.

IT is moste manifest in all the workes of Nature, or creatures that God hath made, that whatsoeuer qualitie, propertie, or vertue is founde in them, by creation, that is to bee holden for their owne. And he that shall, by imagination or coniecture, goe about to take these their properties from them and attribute the same to any other subiects whereunto they appertaine not, I say that man offendeth God muche, for not beleeuing his power to bee sufficient in hys creatures.

I will not offer to dispute with the Logitians in so many poinctes as heere they myght seeme to ouer reach me, in naturall causes. But that this stone hath wholy and fully in himselfe power, action, propertie & vertue of his owne appetite, to shew and to cause the Needle to shewe the point Respectiue, without anie Attractiue qualitie, or external cause of Rockes of the Magnes Stone, or by Attraction in the heauens, or else where whatsoeuer, it is already sufficiently proued.

Notwithstanding, if these proofes may not content, I will at any time required heerein, satisfie the doubtfull by manyfest experimentes. And therfore where no other cause can be probablie anexed vnto this stone, the power and action of necessitie is proued in it selfe.

And by the Declining of the Needle, is also proued, that the poinct Respectiue is rather in the earth then in the heauens as some haue imagined: and the greatest reason why they so thought, as I iudge, was because they neuer were acquainted with this Declining in ẏ Needle, which doubtlesse if Martin Curtes had knowen, hee woulde not haue iudged the Attractiue poinct to haue beene in the heauens, or without them, but rather in the earth.

Now peraduenture you will aske me howe this Stone hath his power, and how it is ingendred: I am no more able to satisfie you heerein, then if you should aske me howe

and

and by what meanes the celestiall spheres are mooued: but that God in his omnipotent prouidence hath appointed it so to be: which may serue for a generall answer, to all such curious searchers of the secret woorkes of God in his creatures. As though his worde alone were not a sufficient decrée and lawe to all his woorkes: but binding them to second causes, as a thing of necessitie.

These curious searchers out of the secretes of nature, further then is requisite that man should knowe for his necessarie vse, I may compare to Esdras, and wishe them to read ouer his fourth booke, and there they shall see how he was answered at Gods handes by his Angell, for his curious questions asked and demaunded.

Nowe therefore, as I haue before declared, that dyuers haue whetted their wits, yea, and dulled them, as I haue mine, and yet in the end haue beene constrained to flie to the corner Stone, I meane God, who (to conclude) hath giuen vertue and power to this Stone, proper in it selfe, to shewe one certaine poinct, by his owne nature and appetite, and not subiecte to any other accident in heauen, nor in earth, but freely by his owne proper vertue receiued at his mightie handes in creation: and by the same vertue the Needle is turned vpon his owne Center, I meane the Center of his Circular and inuisible vertue, pearcing all thinges and staied by nothing, bée it wall, boord, glasse, or any thing whatsoeuer.

And surely I am of opinion, that if this vertue coulde by any meanes be made visible to the eie of man, it woulde bée found in a Sphericall forme extending rounde about the Stone in great compasse, and the deade bodie of the Stone in the middest thereof, whose Center is the Center of hys aforesaide vertue. And this I haue partly proued and made visible to be seene in some manner, and God sparing mee lyfe, I will héerein make further experience, and that not curiouslie, but in the feare of God, as néere as he shall giue me grace, and meane to annexe the same vnto a booke of

Nauiga-

Nauigation, which I haue had long in hand.

The nienth Chapter.

Of the Variation of the Needle, from the pole or Axeltree of the earth, and how it is to be vnderstood.

NOW, as the Needle hath this apparant propertie in Declining vnder the Horizon, to shew the point Respectiue: So it is most manifest that as in Declining it hath a property in varying, or departing from the Poles, euen as the point Respectiue openeth, or sheweth a greater, or lesser distance betwixt the said point Respectiue, and the Pole or Axeltree of the earth. And this departing is called Variation of the Needle. This is also shewed in the Needle or wier, in that conclusion of declyning in the water, as in the first Chapter, euen by the same proportion, that it sheweth in the Needle Horizontally.

This Variation is no other thing, then a certaine parte or portion of a circle, contained betwixt two straight lines proceeding both from one Center, which may be imagined to be the Center of the Needle, and from thence both extending and going directly forth, one to the Pole or Axeltree of the world, and the other to the point Respectiue, and this part of circle contained betwixt these two lines in the Horizon, is said to be Variation.

And further here is to be noted, that alwaies these two lines haue two right lynes, cutting them directly in the Center of the needle. The one of them crossing the Miridian at right angles in the Center of the needle, is the true East and West of the worlde. And the other crossing the line Respectiue at right angles, is the false East and west that the varying Needle or Compasse sheweth: all which is shewed by this present figure following.

This

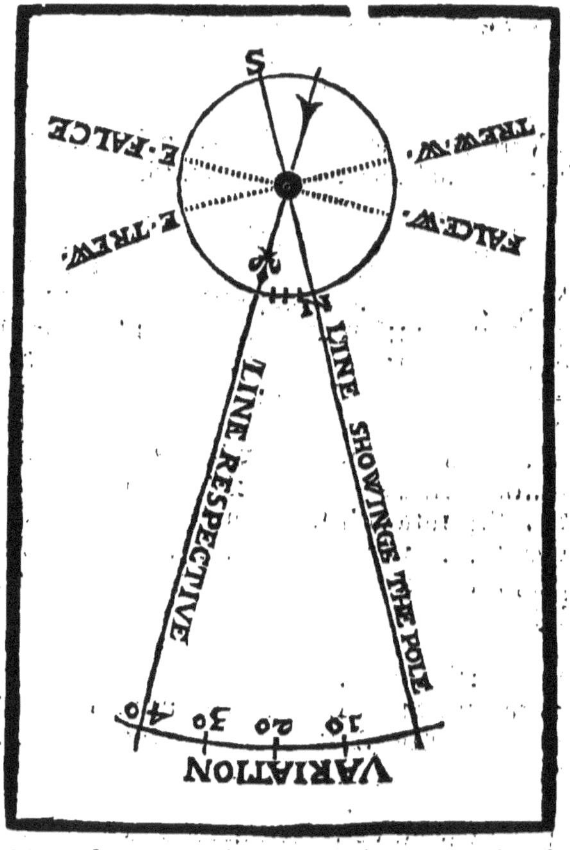

This Variation is iudged by diuers trauailers to bee by equall proportion, but heerein they are much deceiued, and therefore it appeareth that notwithstanding their trauaile, they haue more followed their bookes then experience in that matter. True it is, that Martin Curtes doth allowe it to bee by proportion, but it is a moste false and erronious rule. For there is neither proportion nor vniformitie in it, but in some places swift and sudden, and in some places slowe.

It

It is said to be proportionall or uniforme, when in the increasing or decreasing of a degree of Variation, is found one certaine number of leagues or miles, going, increasing or decreasing in one Paralell or Latitude, by like equall proportion, and that if the Variation be doubled, going by one paralel, so shall the leagues or miles also. But this is not found to be so.

For in going from Sillie to Newfound-land, which is not 600. Leagues, it is found that the Needle doeth varie more in 200. Leagues, when you come neere that Countrie, then it doth in 400. Leagues of your first way. And also going to Meta Incognita, it varieth more in parte of the last of the way, the in ⅓ of the firste: and in those partes it is found to bee sodaine. Further it is found betweene the North Cape and Vaigatz verie strange, in recoyling and comming backe againe to the Westwardes of the Pole before it hath fullie accomplished two pointes of variation in the compasse. So that at Vaigatz it varieth to the Westwardes, as it doth at Newfound-land. And this comming backe againe, before it hath accomplished four pointes of the Compasse, is verie strange, and against the opinions of all that haue before written.

Because the line of the Needle that sheweth the Pole Artik, and point Respectiue, by vertue of the stone passeth betweene Silly and Newfound-land.

Pedro de Medina (as I haue said in the seconde Chapter) was doubtfull of the Variation, saying: that if the Compasse did varie, the faulte might bee in the making thereof, the wiers or Needle not being well placed. yet he was a learned man, and a great traueller to the West Indies. But it appeareth that he had no more regard to the Variation, then many Mariners in these daies.

For in 18, or 20. yeares that I haue trauailed, the seas beeing dayly conuersant with many of them, and diligent in enquiring of Variation of the places, where I haue not beene my selfe, I could neuer finde two of them in one trueth, except for the trauailes from hence Northwardes, and North Eastwardes. But I suppose the greatest occasion thereof is by lacke of exacte Instrumentes for

that

that purpose. Wherefore I haue deuised one verie necessarie.

And further because this variation is diuers, and is found sometimes to the Eastwards, and sometimes to the Westwardes of the Pole, I wil declare what the variatiō is heere in London, by mine owne obseruation, and in other places, as I haue groslie gathered of some trauellers, reckoning, or beginning at the ancient bound or great Meridian that passeth by the Ile of Saynt Michaell in the Asores, where it is said, that the Néedle sheweth directly the Pole, and the Respectiue point both in one line. But this is not found to be so.

True it is, that the North point of the common Compasse sheweth the Pole verie neere in that Meridian, but the bare Néedle sheweth about 4. deg. 50. min. to the eastwards of the Pole. So that you must vnderstand alwaies, the difference betweene the common Compasse & the Needle to be at the least ½ part of a point, and of some more: because the greatest part of the common sailing Compasses hath the Needle set in the Flye, halfe a point, or ½ to the Eastwardes of the North, and some ¾ of a point, and others at a whole point, and some againe are set directlie vnder the Flowerde Luce, or North of the Compasse, these are called Meridionall Compasses, because they shew directly the Pole in the great Meridian, as the bare Néedle doth, which Meridian must needes bée at the least 100. or 120. leagues to the Westwards of the Ile of Saint Michaell.

And therefore to write of the Variation of places by the common reportes of Mariners that haue trauelled Southwards and Westwards from hence, it shall bee as vncertaine, as are the diuers makinges of these common compasses, by which they haue made their obseruations. And therefore I will omit it, and speake onely of this place or Cittie of London, whose latitude I finde to bee 51. degrees, 32. min. and the Variation of the Needle from this

Meridi-

Meridian of the Pole to be 11. degrées. 15. minutes.

And although this Variation of the Néedle, bée found in trauaile to be diuers and changeable, yet at anie Lande or fixed place assigned, it remaineth alwaies one, still permanent and abiding. And therefore I wish the Maryner to make diligent obseruation of thys Variation in dyuers places, as hee shall trauaile, by some exact Instruments for the purpose. For it may be greatly for his aid, against hee come there another time, especially in such places where the variation is swift, as in these North partes. And because the common Compasse is pertaker of this Variation and Declyning, as the Needle is, I will somewhat shewe of the sundrie sortes and makings of them, with the inconueniences that may growe by them, and by yll plats made by these diuers sortes of Compasses.

The tenth Chapter.

Of the common Compasses, and of the diuers different sorts & makings of them with the inconueniences that may grow by them, and the plats made by them.

Of these common sayling Compasses, I find hée in Europa fiue sundrie sorts or sets. The first is of Leuant made in Sycile, Genoua and Venice: and these are al for the most part made meridionally with the Wyers directlye set vnder the South and North of the Compasse and therefore duelye shewing the point Respectiue in all places, as the bare Needle, and by this compasse are the Plats made, for the most part of all the Leuant Seas.

Secondly, there are made in Danske, in the Sound of

Denmarke, and in Flanders, that haue the wiers set at ½ of a point to the Eastwards of the North of the Compasse, and also some at a whole point, and by these compasses they make both the plats, and Rutters for the sound.

Thirdly, there hath beene made in this Countrey particularlie for Saint Nicholas and Russia, Compasses set at ½ of a point, and the first plats of that discouerie were made by this Compasse.

Fourthly, the Compasse made at Seuill, Lisbone, Rochell, Bourdeaux, Roan, and heere in England, are moste commonly set at halfe a point, and by this Compasse are the plats of the East and West Indies made for their Pylots, and also for our coastes neere heerby, as France, Spain, Portugall, and England: and therefore best of these Nations to bee vsed, because it is the most common sorte that is generally vsed in these coastes. And againe, it is said, that the middle hazard is best.

I speake thus, because there are so many sortes of these Compasses different each from other, as before I haue declared: And the Maister or Mariner sayling by these Compasses of sundry sortes, may thereby fall into great perrill, and the reason is, because that of long tyme these compasses haue beene vsed, and by them the Marine Plats haue beene described of sundry sorts, euerie one according to the compasse of that countrie.

If then hee take not the Compasse of the same sette or making that the plat was made my, then his Card or plat will shewe him one course: and the compasse when hee thinketh hee goeth well, will carrie him another way. And thus, when hee thinketh to fall with the place that his Card sheweth him, he shall bee as farre wide, as the Compasse he hath sailed by, is different from that his plat was made by.

This is the grounde and cause of many inconueniences, which is now too late to bee generally reformed: therfore I wish the Marriner to haue a greate regarde vnto this,

this, as a principall point in Nauigation, and not to saile by a Compasse of one parish, & a plat of another: I meane that they haue a respect, as neere as they may, to sayle by a Compasse of that countrie where his plat was made.

Yet manie there are that vse our Compasse with Leuant Plats: but I suppose, without good consideration therein, they shall make but wide reckonings. And this hath beene sufficientlie of late experimented, by our Mariners, that haue vsed Leuant.

Peraduenture there are some will say, that he knoweth a good Compasse, if he see it. I say the Compasse may be good, and yet not good for him, except his plat bee agreeable: As for example, a Leuant Compasse is a good Compasse to vse with a Leuant Plat, but it differeth from our compasse halfe a poinct more Easterlie. And others there are of Danske, that differ from ours ½ a point more Westerlie, and yet being vsed in their kind, are good compasses.

And therefore I conclude, that generally the best compasse is this sorte set at ½ a poinct, because the maior parte of Compasses and Plats, dooth not differ from this aboue ¼ of a poinct, except the two aboue named of Leuant and Danske.

I haue heard many say, that haue trauelled farre to the Southwardes, that the Compasse hath seemed to loose his force, and to waxe weake and dull. I iudge the cause is not by reason of the farre distance from the North Pole, but rather by beeing long absent from the Stone, for not beeing touched or refreshed therewith. And againe, the Pinne that beareth the Flie, may bee so dulled with long vsing, that the Flie is as it were staied, that it cannot play as it would, if it were sharpe.

Therefore, if you make it sharpe with a Whetstone, you shall finde it remedied: and also when you finde it light, or too tyckle, you may dull the poinct of the Pinne, with the leafe of a paire of writing tables, vntill you may see the toppe thereof, and then the Compasse will bee better for a high Sea. And thus by sharping and dulling of the Pinne, you may make your compasse fit for all Weathers.

HEERE AFTER FOLloweth a table of the Sunnes Declination, commonly called a Regiment for the Sunne, axactly calculated vnto the minute by the true place of the Sun, whose greatest declination for this age, is 23. Degrees 28 minutes, and may serue for 30. yeares without great errour.

Ianuary.

Leap yeare.			First.			Second.			Third.		
4			1			2			3		
1596			1597			1598			1599		
1600			1601			1602			1603		
1604			1605			1606			1607		
1608			1609			1610			1611		
1612			1613			1614			1615		
D	G	M	D	G	M	D	G	M	D	G	M
1	21	57	1	21	50	1	21	52	1	21	56
2	21	47	2	21	40	2	21	34	2	21	45
3	21	36	3	21	30	3	21	33	3	21	36
4	21	25	4	21	20	4	21	23	4	21	26
5	21	15	5	21	9	5	21	13	5	21	15
6	21	5	6	20	59	6	21	0	6	21	4
7	20	54	7	20	48	7	20	50	7	20	54
8	20	43	8	20	36	8	20	38	8	20	41
9	20	31	9	20	23	9	20	26	9	20	29
10	20	20	10	20	10	10	20	[illegible]	10	20	16
11	20	6	11	19	59	11	20	0	11	20	3
12	19	52	12	19	43	12	19	47	12	19	53
13	19	35	13	19	30	13	19	33	13	19	39
14	19	23	14	19	14	14	19	19	14	19	25
15	19	7	15	19	0	15	19	4	15	19	12
16	18	54	16	18	45	16	18	49	16	18	56
17	18	39	17	18	29	17	18	34	17	18	41
18	18	23	18	18	14	18	18	10	18	18	26
19	18	8	19	17	58	19	18	2	19	18	11
20	17	52	20	17	42	20	17	46	20	17	54
21	17	36	21	17	25	21	17	32	21	17	38
22	17	19	22	17	8	22	17	12	22	17	21
23	17	4	23	16	51	23	16	56	23	17	4
24	16	45	24	16	32	24	16	38	24	16	47
25	16	28	25	16	16	25	16	21	25	16	29
26	16	10	26	15	57	26	16	3	26	16	12
27	15	53	27	15	39	27	15	45	27	15	49
28	15	33	28	15	21	28	15	20	28	15	30
29	15	15	29	15	2	29	15	7	29	15	12
30	14	56	30	14	43	30	14	48	30	14	53
31	14	35	31	14	24	31	14	29	31	14	34

South declination.

South declination.

South declination.

Februarie.

Leap yeare.			First.			Second.			third.		
4			1			2			3		
1596 1600 1604 1608 1612			1597 1601 1605 1609 1613			1598 1602 1606 1610 1614			1599 1603 1607 1611 1615		
D	G	M	D	G	M	D	G	M	D	G	M
1	14	19	1	14	4	1	14	10	1	14	14
2	14	0	2	13	44	2	13	50	2	13	54
3	13	40	3	13	24	3	13	30	3	13	35
4	13	20	4	13	4	4	13	9	4	13	16
5	13	0	5	12	43	5	12	49	5	12	57
9	12	40	6	12	23	6	12	29	6	12	34
7	12	19	7	12	2	7	12	8	7	12	14
8	11	58	8	11	41	8	11	47	8	11	52
9	11	37	9	11	20	9	11	26	9	11	32
10	11	16	10	10	58	10	11	4	10	11	12
11	10	55	11	10	36	11	10	43	11	10	50
12	10	30	12	10	15	12	10	21	12	10	28
13	10	10	13	9	53	13	9	59	13	10	6
14	9	49	14	9	31	14	9	37	14	9	43
15	9	27	15	9	9	15	9	14	15	9	21
16	9	5	16	8	47	16	8	50	16	8	58
17	8	43	17	8	24	17	8	28	17	8	36
18	8	21	18	8	2	18	8	6	18	8	14
19	7	58	19	7	39	19	7	44	19	7	50
20	7	36	20	7	16	20	7	21	20	7	28
21	7	13	21	6	53	21	6	54	21	7	5
22	6	50	22	6	30	22	6	32	22	6	42
23	6	27	23	6	7	23	6	10	23	6	19
24	6	3	24	5	44	24	5	48	24	5	56
25	5	40	25	5	21	25	5	24	25	5	32
26	5	18	26	4	58	25	5	2	26	5	8
27	4	53	27	4	34	27	4	39	27	4	44
28	4	31	28	4	10	28	4	14	28	4	21
29	4	6									

South declination. South declination. South declination.

March.														
Leap yeare.				First.				Second.				Third.		
4				1				2				3		
1596 1600 1604 1608 1612				1597 1601 1605 1609 1613				1598 1602 1606 1610 1614				1599 1603 1607 1611 1615		
D	G	M		D	G	M		D	G	M		D	G	M
1	3	43	South declination.	1	3	47	South declination.	1	3	53	South declination.	1	3	59
2	3	19		2	3	24		2	3	29		2	3	35
3	2	56		3	3	0		3	3	6		3	3	12
4	2	32		4	2	36		4	2	42		4	2	48
5	2	9		5	2	13		5	2	18		5	2	25
6	1	45		6	1	49		6	1	55		9	2	1
7	1	22		7	1	25		7	1	31		7	1	37
8	0	59		8	1	2		8	1	11		8	1	14
9	0	34		9	0	39		9	0	47		9	0	50
10	0	11	Equi	10	0	15	nocti	10	0	20	all.	10	0	26
11	0	12		11	0	8		11	0	3		11	0	3
12	0	36		12	0	32		12	0	27		12	0	21
13	0	59	North declination.	13	0	56	North declination.	13	0	51	North declination.	13	0	44
14	1	23		14	1	19		14	1	14		14	1	8
15	1	46		15	1	43		15	1	37		15	1	31
16	2	10		16	2	6		16	2	1		16	1	55
17	2	33		17	2	30		17	2	24		17	2	18
18	2	56		18	2	54		18	2	48		18	2	41
19	3	20		19	3	17		19	3	11		19	3	5
20	3	43		20	3	41		20	3	34		20	3	28
21	4	6		21	4	3		21	3	57		21	3	52
22	4	29		22	4	27		22	4	21		22	4	15
23	4	52		23	4	50		23	4	44		23	4	38
24	5	15		24	5	13		24	5	7		24	5	1
25	5	38		25	5	36		25	5	30		25	5	24
26	6	1		26	5	59		26	5	53		26	5	47
27	6	23		27	6	21		27	6	15		27	6	10
28	6	46		28	6	44		28	6	38		28	6	33
29	7	8		29	7	6		29	7	1		29	6	56
30	7	30		30	7	29		30	7	23		30	7	19
31	7	52		31	7	51		31	7	45		31	7	42

April.

Leap yeare.			First.			Second.			Third.		
4			1			2			3		
1596 1600 1604 1608 1612			1597 1601 1605 1609 1613			1598 1602 1606 1610 1614			1599 1603 1607 1611 1615		
D	G	M	D	G	M	D	G	M	D	G	M
1	8	15	1	8	13	1	8	8	1	8	10
2	8	37	2	8	35	2	8	30	2	8	25
3	8	58	3	8	57	3	8	52	3	8	47
4	9	19	4	9	19	4	9	14	4	9	9
5	9	41	5	9	41	5	9	36	5	9	30
6	10	2	9	10	2	6	9	57	6	9	52
7	10	23	7	10	23	7	10	18	7	10	13
8	10	44	8	10	44	8	10	40	8	10	34
9	11	6	9	11	5	9	11	1	9	10	55
10	11	25	10	11	25	10	11	21	10	11	16
11	11	46	11	11	45	11	11	42	11	11	36
12	12	6	12	12	6	12	12	2	12	11	56
13	12	26	13	12	26	13	12	22	13	12	16
14	12	46	14	12	46	14	12	45	14	12	36
15	13	5	15	13	6	15	13	3	15	12	56
16	13	25	16	13	25	16	13	23	16	13	16
17	13	44	17	13	44	17	13	42	17	13	35
18	14	3	18	14	4	18	14	1	18	13	55
19	14	22	19	14	22	19	14	20	19	14	14
20	14	40	20	14	41	20	14	38	20	14	32
21	14	59	21	14	59	21	14	58	21	14	51
22	15	17	22	15	17	22	15	15	22	15	9
23	15	35	23	15	35	23	15	33	23	15	27
24	15	52	24	15	53	24	15	50	24	15	45
25	16	9	25	16	10	25	15	8	25	16	2
26	16	27	26	16	27	26	16	25	26	16	19
27	16	43	27	16	44	27	16	42	27	16	36
28	17	0	28	17	1	28	16	58	28	16	53
29	17	16	29	17	17	29	17	14	29	17	9
30	17	32	30	17	33	30	17	30	30	17	26

North declination.

North declination.

North declination.

May.

Leap yeare.			First.			Second.			third.		
4			1			2			3		
1596			1597			1598			1599		
1600			1601			1602			1603		
1604			1605			1606			1607		
1608			1609			1610			1611		
1612			1613			1614			1615		
D	G	M	D	G	M	D	G	M	D	G	M
1	17	48	1	17	49	1	17	45	1	17	48
2	18	3	2	17	57	2	18	1	2	18	3
3	18	18	3	18	12	3	18	16	3	18	18
4	18	33	4	18	27	4	18	31	4	18	33
5	18	48	5	18	41	5	18	45	5	18	48
6	19	2	6	18	56	6	19	0	6	19	3
7	19	16	7	19	9	7	19	13	7	19	17
8	19	29	8	19	23	8	19	27	8	19	31
9	19	42	9	19	36	9	19	40	9	19	43
10	19	56	10	19	49	10	19	53	10	19	56
11	20	8	11	20	2	11	20	6	11	20	8
12	20	20	12	20	14	12	20	17	12	20	20
13	20	32	13	20	26	13	20	30	13	20	32
14	20	43	14	20	38	14	20	41	14	20	42
15	20	54	15	20	49	15	20	53	15	20	54
16	21	5	16	21	0	16	21	4	16	21	5
17	21	16	17	21	10	17	21	14	17	21	16
18	21	26	18	21	20	18	21	24	18	21	26
19	21	35	19	21	30	19	21	34	19	21	32
20	21	45	20	21	39	20	21	43	20	21	[illegible]
21	21	54	21	21	49	21	21	52	21	21	50
22	22	2	22	21	57	22	22	0	22	21	59
23	22	10	23	22	6	23	22	8	23	22	7
24	22	18	24	22	14	24	22	16	24	22	15
25	22	25	25	22	21	25	22	24	25	22	22
26	22	33	26	22	28	26	22	32	26	22	30
27	22	39	27	22	35	27	22	40	27	22	36
28	22	45	28	22	41	28	22	[illegible]	28	22	42
29	22	51	26	22	47	29	22	[illegible]	29	22	48
30	22	56	32	22	52	30	22	[illegible]	30	22	54
[illegible]	[illegible]	[illegible]	31	22	[illegible]	31	22	[illegible]	31	22	58

North declination.

North declination.

North declination.

Iune.

Leap yeare.				First.				Second.				Third.		
4				1				2				3		
1596 1600 1604 1608 1612				1597 1601 1605 1609 1613				1598 1602 1606 1610 1614				1599 1603 1607 1611 1615		
D	G	M		D	G	M		D	G	M		D	G	M
1	23	0		1	23	4		1	23	4		1	23	3
2	23	7		2	23	9		2	23	8		2	23	7
3	23	12		3	23	13		3	23	12		3	23	11
4	23	16		4	23	16		4	23	16		4	23	15
5	23	19		5	23	19		5	23	20		5	23	18
6	23	22		6	23	22		6	23	22		6	23	21
7	23	24		7	23	24		7	23	23		7	23	23
8	23	26		8	23	26		8	23	25		8	23	25
9	23	27		9	23	27		9	23	26		9	23	26
10	23	28	North tropick. declination.	10	23	28	North tropick. declination.	10	23	27	North tropick. declination.	10	23	27
11	23	28		11	23	28		11	23	28		11	23	28
12	23	28		12	23	28		12	23	28		12	23	28
13	23	28		13	23	28		13	23	28		13	23	28
14	23	27		14	23	27		14	23	28		14	23	27
15	23	25		15	23	26		15	23	26		15	23	26
16	23	23		16	23	24		16	23	25		16	23	25
17	23	22		17	23	22		17	23	23		17	23	23
18	23	18		18	23	19		18	23	22		18	23	21
19	23	15		19	23	16		19	23	17		19	23	18
20	23	12		20	23	13		20	23	14		20	23	15
21	23	8		21	23	9		21	23	10		21	23	11
22	23	4		22	23	5		22	23	6		22	23	7
23	22	59		23	23	1		23	23	2		23	23	4
24	22	54		24	22	56		24	22	57		24	22	58
25	22	49		25	22	51		25	22	52		25	22	53
26	22	43		26	22	45		26	22	47		26	22	48
27	22	39		27	22	38		27	22	40		27	22	41
28	22	30		28	22	33		28	22	34		28	22	35
29	22	23		29	22	25		29	22	27		29	32	26
30	22	15		30	22	18		30	22	20		30	22	21

Iuly.

Leap yeare. 4			First. 1			Second. 2			Third. 3		
1596			1597			1598			1599		
1600			1601			1602			1603		
1604			1605			1606			1607		
1608			1609			1610			1611		
1612			1613			1614			1615		
D	G	M	D	G	M	D	G	M	D	G	M
1	22	12	1	22	10	1	22	14	1	22	2[illegible]
2	22	4	2	22	[illegible]	2	22	4	2	32	6
3	21	5[illegible]	3	21	54	3	21	56	3	21	58
4	21	47	4	21	45	4	21	47	4	21	49
5	21	[illegible]3	5	21	35	5	21	38	5	21	40
6	21	28	6	21	26	6	21	28	6	21	30
7	21	19	7	21	16	7	21	19	7	21	21
8	21	[illegible]	8	21	6	8	21	6	8	21	11
9	20	5[illegible]	9	20	55	9	20	58	9	21	0
10	20	4[illegible]	10	20	44	10	20	47	10	20	49
11	20	29	11	20	33	11	20	36	11	20	38
12	20	17	12	20	21	12	20	24	12	20	26
13	20	5	13	20	9	13	20	12	13	20	14
14	19	52	14	19	57	14	20	0	14	20	6
15	19	41	15	19	44	15	19	47	15	19	49
16	19	27	16	19	31	16	19	34	16	19	36
17	19	13	17	19	17	17	19	20	17	19	23
18	18	59	18	19	4	18	19	7	18	19	10
19	18	45	19	18	4[illegible]	19	18	53	19	18	56
20	18	31	20	18	35	20	18	38	20	18	43
21	18	16	21	18	21	21	18	24	21	18	28
22	18	1	22	18	6	22	18	9	22	18	13
23	17	47	23	17	51	23	17	54	23	17	58
24	17	30	24	17	35	24	17	38	24	17	42
25	17	14	25	17	19	25	17	23	25	17	26
26	16	58	26	17	[illegible]	26	17	6	26	17	11
27	16	42	27	16	4[illegible]	27	16	50	27	16	55
28	16	25	28	16	30	28	16	33	28	16	38
29	15	8	29	16	13	29	16	17	29	16	21
30	15	51	30	15	56	30	16	0	30	16	4
31	15	33	31	15	39	31	15	4[illegible]	31	15	47

North declination.

North declination.

North declination.

August.

Leap yeare.			First.			Second.			Third.		
4			1			2			3		
1596			1597			1598			1599		
1600			1601			1602			1603		
1604			1605			1606			1607		
1608			1609			1610			1611		
1612			1613			1614			1615		
D	G	M	D	G	M	D	G	M	D	G	M
1	15	15	1	15	21	1	15	25	1	15	30
2	14	57	2	15	3	2	15	7	2	15	12
3	14	39	3	14	45	3	14	49	3	14	54
4	14	20	4	14	27	4	14	31	4	14	36
5	14	2	5	14	8	5	14	12	5	14	18
6	13	43	9	13	49	6	13	53	6	13	59
7	13	24	7	13	30	7	13	34	7	13	40
8	13	5	8	13	9	8	13	15	8	13	20
9	12	41	9	12	51	9	12	56	9	13	2
10	12	25	10	12	31	10	12	36	10	12	42
11	12	5	11	12	12	11	12	16	11	12	23
12	11	45	12	11	52	12	11	56	12	12	3
13	11	25	13	11	32	13	11	36	13	11	42
14	11	4	14	11	11	14	11	16	14	11	22
15	10	44	15	10	51	15	10	59	15	11	2
16	10	23	16	10	30	16	10	35	16	10	41
17	10	2	17	10	9	17	10	14	17	10	20
18	9	41	18	9	48	18	9	53	18	9	59
19	9	19	19	9	27	19	9	31	19	9	39
20	8	58	20	9	5	20	9	10	20	9	16
21	8	35	21	8	44	21	8	49	21	8	15
22	8	15	22	8	22	22	8	27	22	8	33
23	7	53	23	8	0	23	8	5	23	8	11
24	7	31	24	7	38	24	7	43	24	7	50
25	7	9	25	7	16	25	7	21	25	7	28
26	6	47	26	6	53	26	6	59	26	7	5
27	6	25	27	6	31	27	6	36	27	6	43
28	6	1	28	6	9	28	6	14	28	6	20
29	5	39	29	5	46	29	5	51	29	5	57
30	5	16	30	5	23	30	5	29	30	5	3[illegible]
31	4	53	31	5	0	31	5	6	31	5	12

North declination.

North declination.

North declination.

September.

Leap yeare.			First.			Second.			Third.		
4			1			2			3		
1596 1600 1604 1608 1612			1597 1601 1605 1609 1613			1598 1602 1606 1610 1614			1599 1603 1607 1611 1615		
D	G	M	D	G	M	D	G	M	D	G	M
1	4	43	1	4	38	1	4	42	1	4	49
2	4	20	2	4	14	2	4	20	2	4	26
3	3	57	3	3	51	3	3	56	3	4	3
4	3	34	4	3	28	4	3	33	4	3	39
5	3	12	5	3	5	5	3	10	5	3	16
6	2	47	6	2	37	6	2	47	9	2	53
7	2	24	7	2	18	7	2	23	7	2	29
8	2	1	8	1	55	8	2	0	8	2	6
9	1	37	9	1	31	9	1	37	9	1	43
10	1	14	10	1	8	10	1	13	10	1	19
11	0	51	11	0	45	11	0	49	11	0	56
12	0	27	12	0	21	12	0	26	12	0	52
13	0	3	13	0	21	13	0	3	13	0	9
14	0	20	14	0	25	14	0	21	14	0	15
15	0	43	15	0	48	15	0	44	15	0	38
16	1	7	16	1	12	16	1	8	16	1	2
17	1	30	17	1	35	17	1	31	17	1	25
18	1	54	18	1	58	18	1	55	18	1	48
19	2	17	19	2	22	19	2	18	19	2	12
20	2	41	20	2	45	20	2	45	20	2	35
21	3	4	21	3	9	21	3	5	21	2	59
22	3	27	22	3	32	22	3	28	22	3	22
23	3	50	23	3	55	23	3	51	23	3	45
24	4	14	24	4	18	24	4	15	24	4	9
25	4	37	25	4	41	25	4	38	25	4	32
26	5	0	26	5	4	26	5	1	26	4	55
27	5	23	27	5	27	27	5	23	27	5	18
28	5	46	28	5	51	28	5	46	28	5	41
29	6	8	29	6	14	29	6	9	29	6	4
30	6	31	30	6	36	30	6	32	30	6	26

North declination. North declination. North declination.

Equi noctiall.

South declination. South declination. South declination.

October.

Leap yeare.			First.			Second.			Third.		
4			1			2			3		
1596 1600 1604 1608 1612			1597 1601 1605 1609 1613			1598 1602 1606 1610 1614			1599 1603 1607 1611 1615		
D	G	M	D	G	M	D	G	M	D	G	M
1	6	53	1	7	0	1	6	54	1	6	48
2	7	16	2	7	22	2	7	17	2	7	11
3	7	38	3	7	44	3	7	39	3	7	33
4	8	1	4	8	7	4	8	1	4	7	55
5	8	23	5	8	29	5	8	24	5	8	18
6	8	45	9	8	51	6	8	46	6	8	40
7	9	7	7	9	13	7	9	8	7	9	2
8	9	30	8	9	36	8	9	30	8	9	29
9	9	52	9	9	58	9	9	52	9	9	42
10	10	13	10	10	19	10	10	13	10	10	8
11	10	35	11	10	41	11	10	35	11	10	29
12	10	56	12	11	2	12	11	0	12	10	51
13	11	17	13	11	23	13	11	18	13	11	12
14	11	39	14	11	45	14	11	39	14	11	33
15	11	59	15	12	5	15	12	0	15	11	54
16	12	20	16	12	26	16	12	21	16	12	15
17	12	41	17	12	47	17	12	41	17	12	36
18	13	1	18	13	7	18	13	1	18	12	56
19	13	21	19	13	27	19	13	22	19	13	17
20	13	41	20	13	47	20	13	41	20	13	36
21	14	1	21	14	6	21	14	1	21	13	56
22	14	17	22	14	26	22	14	21	22	14	16
23	14	39	23	14	45	23	14	40	23	14	35
24	14	58	24	15	4	24	14	59	24	14	54
25	15	17	25	15	23	25	15	17	25	15	13
26	15	35	26	15	41	26	15	36	26	15	31
27	15	54	27	[illegible]	59	27	15	54	27	15	50
28	16	12	28	16	17	28	16	12	28	16	8
29	16	29	29	16	35	29	16	30	29	16	25
30	16	47	30	16	52	30	16	47	30	16	43
31	17	4	31	17	9	31	17	4	31	17	0

South declination.

South declination.

South declination.

Nouember.

Leap yeare.			First.			Second.			third.		
4			1			2			3		
1596			1597			1598			1599		
1600			1601			1602			1603		
1604			1605			1606			1607		
1608			1609			1610			1611		
1612			1613			1614			1615		
D	G	M	D	G	M	D	G	M	D	G	M
1	17	3[illegible]	1	17	26	1	17	21	1	17	17
2	17	5[illegible]	2	17	42	2	17	38	2	17	33
3	18	[illegible]	[illegible]	17	58	3	17	54	3	17	49
4	18	2[illegible]	4	18	14	4	18	9	4	18	[illegible]
5	18	4[illegible]	5	18	29	5	18	25	5	18	2[illegible]
6	18	[illegible]	6	18	44	6	18	40	6	18	37
7	19	[illegible]	7	18	59	7	18	55	7	18	52
8	19	24	8	19	14	8	19	10	8	19	6
9	19	38	9	19	26	9	19	24	9	19	21
10	19	5[illegible]	10	19	42	10	19	36	10	19	35
11	20	5	11	19	45	11	19	52	11	19	48
12	20	18	12	20	8	12	20	5	12	20	4
13	20	30	13	20	21	[illegible]	[illegible]	8	13	20	14
14	20	4[illegible]	14	20	34	14	[illegible]	0	14	20	27
15	20	54	15	20	46	15	20	42	15	20	39
16	21	6	16	20	57	16	20	54	16	20	51
17	21	17	17	21	8	17	21	5	17	21	3
18	21	27	18	21	19	18	21	16	18	21	14
19	21	37	19	21	29	19	21	27	19	21	24
20	21	47	20	21	39	20	21	37	20	21	35
21	21	56	21	21	49	21	21	47	21	21	44
22	22	5	22	21	58	22	21	56	22	21	54
23	22	14	23	22	7	23	22	5	23	22	3
24	22	21	24	22	15	24	22	14	24	[illegible]	11
25	22	29	25	22	23	25	2	24	25	22	19
26	22	36	26	22	31	26	22	29	26	22	27
27	22	43	27	22	38	27	22	37	27	2	34
28	22	49	28	22	44	28	22	43	28	22	41
29	22	55	26	22	50	29	22	49	29	[illegible]	47
30	23	0	30	22	56	30	22	54	30	22	53

South declination. South declination. South declination.

4			1			2			3		
1596			1597			1598			1599		
1600			1601			1602			1603		
1604			1605			1606			1607		
1608			1609			1610			1611		
1612			1613			1614			1615		
D	G	M	D	G	M	D	G	M	D	G	M
1	23	1	1	23	1	1	23	0	1	23	1
2	23	10	2	23	6	2	23	5	2	23	10
3	23	14	3	23	10	3	23	9	3	23	14
4	23	17	4	23	14	4	23	13	4	23	17
5	23	20	5	23	17	5	23	17	5	23	19
6	23	22	9	23	20	6	23	20	6	13	21
7	23	25	7	23	23	7	23	22	7	23	24
8	23	26	8	23	25	8	23	25	8	23	26
9	23	27	9	23	26	9	23	26	9	23	27
10	23	28	10	23	27	10	23	27	10	23	28
11	23	28	11	23	28	11	23	28	11	23	28
12	23	28	12	23	28	12	23	28	12	23	28
13	23	27	13	23	28	13	23	28	13	23	27
14	23	26	14	23	27	14	23	27	14	23	26
15	23	24	15	23	26	15	23	26	15	23	24
16	23	21	16	23	24	16	23	24	16	23	21
17	23	18	17	23	21	17	23	22	17	23	18
18	23	15	18	23	19	18	23	20	18	23	15
19	23	12	19	23	16	19	23	17	19	23	12
20	23	8	20	23	12	20	23	13	20	23	8
21	23	6	21	23	8	21	23	7	21	23	5
22	22	57	22	23	3	22	23	4	22	22	57
23	22	52	23	22	58	23	22	59	23	22	53
24	22	46	24	22	52	24	22	54	24	22	46
25	22	40	25	22	47	25	22	48	25	22	40
26	22	33	26	22	40	26	22	42	26	22	33
27	22	25	27	22	36	27	22	35	27	22	25
28	22	18	28	22	30	28	22	28	28	22	18
29	22	9	29	22	22	29	22	20	29	22	9
30	22	0	30	22	14	30	22	12	30	22	0
31	21	52	31	22	6	31	22	4	31	21	52

South tropick declination.

South tropick declination.

South tropick declination.

Howe to vse the Suns Declination, for knowing the eleuation of the Pole.

FIrst learne whether the Sunne haue South Declination, or North Declination. Then marke the shadow hee giueth, whether it shewe towardes the Pole he is neerest, or to the contrary.

If the Sunne giue shadow, the same way that he is from the Equinoctiall, hee shall bee betweene you and the Equinoctiall, then take the meridian altitude, and subtract it from 90. vnto the rest, adioyne your Declination for the day, the Summe of both is the eleuation of the Pole, or your distance from the Equinoctiall.

But if the Sun giue the shadowe to the contrarie side of the Equinoctiall that hee is in (that is to say) the Sun in North Declination giue the shadowe Southwardes, or in South Declinations giue the shadowe Northwardes, then either the Equinoctiall shalbee betweene you and the sun, or you in the Equinoctiall, or els you shall bee betweene the Equinoctiall and the sun, which you shall thus know.

Adde vnto your Meridian altitude of the sunne, the Declination for the day, if it amount to lesse then 90. d. so much as wanteth of 90. d. you shall be from the Equinoctiall that way that the shadow goeth.

But if it amount iust to 90. d. you shall be vnder the Equinoctial. If it amount to more then 90. d. so much as is ouer and aboue 90. d. you shalbee from the Eqninoctiall towards the sun, betweene the Equinoctiall and the sun.

And if at any time you shall obserue the suns altitude in your Zenith, then looke what declination it hath, and so much shall you be from the Equinoctiall, on the same side the sunne is in, but if he haue no Declination, then you shall be vnder the Equinoctiall line.

Hereafter followeth three Tables, the firſt is of the Coniunctions of the ſunne and Moone: the ſecond of their oppoſitions, exactly drawen out of Iohannes Stadius Ephemerides: and the third of the Prime and mooueable Feaſtes.

IN the two firſt Tables in euery ſquare of euery Cullum, you ſhall finde noted, three numbers, which haue ſeuerall ſignifications: the firſt number is for the daie of the Moneth, the ſecond for houres, and the third for minutes, of the middle inſtant of time, for the coniunction or oppoſition of the Sunne and Moone.

Ye are to note that the naturall day accounted in theſe tables, beginneth alwaies at the inſtant of noone, or mid-day, and continueth till the next day noone, which is the iuſt time of 24. houres.

Therefore, when you finde the ſeconde number in anie ſquare of the two firſt Tables, to exceede 12. the ſame is to be accounted with the minutes following, (which is the thirde number) for ſo much after midnight, or of the morning, or forenoone of the next day.

The vſe of the Tables.

FIrſt ſeeke in the third Table the Prime, anſwerable to the yeare of our Lorde. Then returne to the Table of Coniunction, or appoſition of the Moone, and in the firſt cullum ſeeke the ſame number of the Prime. Then in the head of the Table, you ſhall ſeek the Moneth, for which you desire to knowe the coniunction or appositi-on: and desending downe the same Cullum, till you come against the Prime specified, in that square you shall finde three numbers noted, the first is for the day of the moneth, the second the houre, and the thirde the minutes to bee ad-ioyned with the houre, for the middle instant of tyme of the coniunction or opposition.

Example.

This yeare 1581. I desire to knowe the day of the Moones Coniunction or Change, in the Moneth of August, I seeke in the third Table (or Table of the mooueable Feasts) for the Prime, and finde it to be 5. with which number I returne unto the first Table, (which is the Table of the coniunction or change) and find the same in the first Cullum. Then I seeke in the head of the Table for August, and descending downe in the same Cullum, till I come to the square which answereth to the Prime 5. I finde therein noted 28—16—45. which signifie that the coniunction is the 28. day of the Moneth, at 16. H—45. M—and because the seconde number exceedeth 12. therefore I say that the coniunction shall bee the 29. day at 4. H—45—M. in the morning.

But if you find in any one square thrée numbers double noted, they doo signifie, that in the same Moneth there is two coniunctions or oppositions, and likewise doo shewe the dayes, houres, and minutes thereof.

If in any square in the Cullum of any moneth in the Table of Coniunction, you finde noted this marke *. the same doth signifie the Ecclipse of the Sunne at the instant of time noted for the coniunction in that moneth.

Likewise, if in any square in the Table of the oppositi-ons or ful Moones, you finde this marke « the same dooth signifie the eclipse of the Moone, at the instant of tyme no-ted in the same square.

Prime.	1	2	3	4	5	6	7	8	9	10
Ianuary.	18 22 10	7 11 10	26 12 53	16 5 0	5 18 20	23 17 50	12 21 30	1 21 10 / 31 16 20	26 16 30	8 21 30
February.	17 16 0	5 23 28	24 23 10	14 14 50	4 6 50	22 7 10	11 15 0		19 16 30	7 12 40
March.	18 6 0	7 12 50	26 10 19	16 0 0	4 16 40	23 17 30	13 5 30	1 10 10	20 3 50	9 4 40
Aprill.	16 22 40	6 3 11	24 22 5	14 9 1	3 1 6	22 1 50	11 17 0	1 1 40	18 19 50	7 20 50
May.	16 14 20 / 30 22 28	5 17 50	24 10 50	13 10 30	2 8 4 / 21 16 30	21 9 1	11 1 50	30 14 20 / 30 0 30	18 9 40	7 12 30
Iune.	15 3 0	4 8 40	23 0 40	12 5 20	30 1 20	19 15 50	9 9 20	28 9 0	6 1 20	6 3 10
Iuly.	14 19 30	3 23 30	22 15 48	11 17 48	29 12 30	18 23 38	8 16 8	27 16 25	16 7 41	5 16 18
August.	13 6 40	2 13 50	21 7 24	10 8 10	28 1 51	17 9 14	6 23 23	26 0 9	14 16 42	4 4 50
September	11 17 20	1 3 40	19 23 12	9 0 16	26 17 50	15 21 25	5 8 5	24 8 40	13 1 25	2 16 4
October.	11 3 20	30 4 30	19 14 50	8 17 50	26 12 8	15 12 415	4 19 12	23 19 3	12 10 24	2 2 29 / 31 12 38
Nouember	9 13 18	28 15 49	18 5 3	7 11 30	25 7 14	14 6 47	3 11 25	22 7 54	10 20 19	29 22 50
December.	8 23 40	28 2 30	17 17 50	7 4 6	15 1 40	14 2 21	3 2 16	21 83 13	10 8 10	29 9 48

Prime.	Ianuarie.	Februarie.	March.	Aprill.	May.	Iune.	Iuly.	August.	September.	October.	Nouember.	December.
	27	29	27	26	26	24	24	23	21	21	19	19
11	21	10	23	13	4	19	10	0	14	2	14	1
	20	0	30	50	30	20	12	33	8	56	42	42
	17	15	16	15	15	13	13	11	10	9	8	7
12	15	23	22	10	23	17	8	21	10	21	9	20
	11	40	10	25	30	24	12	50	50	30	38	12
	6	4	6	4	4	2	2	30	29	28	27	26
13	6	16	3	15	3	18	8	15	6	21	9	21
	30	50	30	40	3	18	19	30	30	0	46	24
	25	23	25	23	22	21	20	19	18	17	19	10
14	8	18	5	13	23	11	23	15	8	23	18	9
	4	30	40	4	[illegible]	50	36	50	20	48	30	50
	14	13	14	13	12	10	10	8	7	6	5	5
15	22	10	20	2	12	21	6	18	9	23	20	14
	30	50	0	30	50	30	30	45	22	50	24	48
	4	2	3	1	30	28	28	26	25	24	23	23
16	9	23	11	21	12	20	4	14	4	20	14	10
	17	40	55	20	32	17	3	40	0	12	30	8
	22	20	22	20	20	18	17	15	14	13	12	12
17	5	21	10	21	5	13	20	23	10	23	13	8
	39	25	50	25	40	6	30	50	47	50	55	32
	11	9	11	10	9	8	7	5	3	3	1	1 | 31
18	5	23	18	2	20	5	12	20	23	10	20	10 | 4
	32	40	10	4	3	32	20	0	50	50	16	30 | 30
	29	28	30	27	28	26	26	24	23	22	20	20
19	23	18	11	23	15	23	12	20	4	12	22	10
	12	42	50	3[illegible]	38	50	0	30	6	3	3[illegible]	36

Prime.	Ianuary.	February.	March.	Aprill.	May.	Iune.	Iuly.	August.	September	October.	Nouembe.	December.
1	5 10 14	3 11 32	3 22 40	2 ☾7 8	1 / 30 15 / 22 0 / 38	29 7 18	28 18 0	27 6 [illegible]	25 21☾ 2	25 14 30	24 9 50	24 5 9
2	22 22 48	21 13 1[illegible]	23 1 10	21 10 1[illegible]	20 17 30	19 0 20	18 7 30	16 16 4	15 2☾ 50	14 16 50	13 9 40	13 4 48
3	12 0 24	10 18 50	12 10 32	10 23 20	10 9 20	8 17 30	8 0 43	6 7 50	4 15 50	4 1 50	2 14 30	2 6 12
4	1 / 30 0 / 19☾ 4 / 6		1 / 31 13 / 5 0 / 30	29 19 30	29 7 3	27 16 30	27 0 49	25 8 40	23 16 40	23 2 42	21 14 22	21 4 17
5	19 20☾ 15	18 30 20	19 6 30	17 22 30	17 30 30	16 2 30	15 14☾ 1	14 0 13	12 9 36	11 18 50	10 4 40	9 15 40
6	8 3☾ 50	6 17 30	8 8 20	6 23 40	6 15 0	5 6 10	4 20 30	3 9 50	1 22 23	1 / 30 9 / 20 50 / 50	29 7 38	28 18 1
7	27 6 30	25 16 10	27 4 0	25 17 30	25 7 30	23 19 50	23 13 5	22 4 17	20 19 7	20 9 15	18 22 15	18 10 0
8	16 20 30	15 6 20	16 16 0	15 1 50	14 12 40	13 0 40	12 14 21	11 5 30	9 21 50	9 14 47	8 7 34	7 22 30
9	6 11 40	4 22 50	5 8 10	3 16 30	3 0 40	1 9 30	30 7 11	28 22 27	27 15 26	27 9 25	26 4 9	25 21 29
10	24 12 0	23 0 9	24 9 40	22 17 20	22 0 20	20 7 [illegible]	19 16 15	18 3 21	16 17 5	16 9 26	15 4 12	14 23 47

Prime.	Ianuarie.	Februarie.	March.	Aprill.	May.	Iune.	Iulie.	August.	September.	October.	Nouember.	December.
	8	12	13	12	11	10	9	7	6	5	4	3
11	18	10	23	9	17	5	7	15	1 ☾	13	5	23
	20	30	30	40	50	40	38	21	10	26	0	10
	3	2	2	1 30	29	2[illegible]	27	25	24	23	20	22
12	12	5	18 ☾	5 13	21	3	15	21 ☾	9	23	18	13
	8	25	40	20 50	19	[illegible]	18	40	50	36	20	30
	21	19	21	20	19	17	17	15	13	13	11	11
13	8	23	16	3	33	21	2	11 ☾	20	0	20	12
	50	0	30	30	10	40	30	25	12	50	30	50
	10	9	10	9	8	7	6	5	3	2	1 30	30
14	8	3	21	12	23	12	20	4	12	20	6 19	9 ☾
	6	20	5	40	50	13	20	11	9	50	35 0	50
	18	17	29	28	27	26	25	24	22	21	20	19
15	23	21	14	7	21	9	19	4	19	22	88	19
	30	22	37	0	7	25	12	30	30	30	7	34
	18	16	17	16	15	14	14	12	10	10	8	8
16	9	23	15	7	23	3 ☾	2	16	23	14	23	10
	36	36	27	35	25	36	30	8	50	30	30	30
	6	5	6	5	4	3	3	1 31	25	29	27	27
17	22	9	20	10	23	15	4	20 10	23	13	23	12
	12	17	11	38	50	25	35	48 30	30	36	50	12
	25	24	25	24	23	22	21	20	19	18	17	16
18	23	10	20	7	19	8	21	12	4	22 ☾	12	23
	50	12	13	13	25	11	30	30	8	16	16	50
	15	14	5	13	13	11	10	9	8	7	4	6
19	15	7	11	20 ☾	5	14	23	12	5	22	16	10
	6	34	30	12	9	53	30	50	30	30	30	8

Heere followeth an Almanacke, whereby may bee knowne the Prime, Epact & Dominicall letter: as also the moueable Feastes for 24. yeares to come. Which Almanacke is to be referred to the Kalender in the beginning of the booke.

Anno Domini.	The prime.	The Epact.	The Sunday letter	Easter daies.	Rogation Sunday.	Ascention day.	Whitson day.	Betwixt Whitsontide and Midsommer. week.	daie
1596	1	11	DC	11. Aprill.	16. May.	20. May.	30. May.	3.	4
1597	2	22	B	27. March.	1. May.	5. May.	15. May.	5.	5
1598	3	3	A	16. April.	21. May.	25. May	4. Iune.	2.	6
1599	4	14	G	8. April.	13. May.	17. May.	27. May.	4.	0
1600	5	25	FE	23. March,	27. Apri	1. May.	11. May.	6.	2
1601	6	6	D	12. April.	17. May.	21. May.	31. May.	3.	3
1602	7	17	C	4. Aprill.	9. May.	12. May.	23. May.	4.	4
1603	8	28	B	24. Aprill.	29. May.	2. Iune.	12. Iune.	1.	5
1604	9	9	AG	8. April.	13. May.	17. May.	27. May.	4.	0
1605	10	20	F	31. March	5. May.	9. May.	19. May.	5.	1
1606	11	1	E	20. April.	25. May.	29. May.	8. Iune.	2.	2
1607	12	12	D	5. April.	10. May.	14. May.	24. May.	4.	3
1608	13	23	CB	27. March	1. May.	5. May.	15. May.	5.	5
1609	14	4	A	16. April.	21. May.	25. May.	4. Iune	2.	6
1610	15	15	G	1. April.	6. May.	10. May.	20 May.	5.	0
1611	16	26	F	24. March	28. Apri	2. May.	12 May.	6.	1
1612	17	7	ED	12. Aprill.	17. May.	21. May.	31. May.	3.	3
1613	18	18	C	4. Aprill.	9. May.	13. May.	23. May.	4.	4
1614	19	29	B	7. April.	22. May.	26 May.	5. Iune.	2.	5
1615	1	11	A	9. April.	14. May.	18. May.	28. May.	3.	6
1616	2	22	GF	31. March	5. May.	9. May.	19. May.	5.	1
1617	3	3	E	13. April.	18. May.	22. May.	1. Iune.	3.	2
1618	4	14	C	5. April.	10. May.	14. May.	24. May	4.	3
1629	5	25	D	28. March.	2. May.	6. May.	15. May.	5.	4

The contents of the Kalender following.

In the first and second Cullum, vnder the title daies, are the daies of the moneth, & dominicall letters, the third is of the feasts: the fourth cullum sheweth howe manie houres and minutes the day containeth from Sun rising to Sun setting, the Pole being eleuated 52. degrées. The fifth cullum of the 27. letters serueth with the help of a Table following, to know what signe the Moone is in at all times.

How by the length of the day is knowen the length of the night, with the houre and minute of the Sunnes rising and setting.

Deuide the length of the day, which you shall finde in the Kalender, into two partes equally, the one halfe sheweth the houres and minutes of the Suns setting, the houres and minutes of the setting, being substracted from 12. the remaine sheweth the houres and minutes of the rising: the whole arke or length of the day, beeing subtracted from 24 the rest sheweth the length of the night (that is to say) from Sunne setting to Sunne rising.

As for example.

The 15. of January, I finde in the Kalender the length of the day to be 8. houres 30 minutes, which beeing deuyded the halfe thereof is 4. houres. 15. minutes. the Sunnes setting that day: this 4. houres, 15. minutes. subtracted from 12. resteth 7. houres, 45. minutes, which is the houre of the Sunnes rising: subtract 8. houres. 30. minutes, the whole length of the day, out of 24. rest 15. houres, 30. minutes, which is the length of the night that day of the moneth.

The

The Kalender.

Dayes.		January.	Length of the daies.		☾
1	A	New yeres day	7	25	b
2	b	Octa. Stephen:	7	55	a
3	c	Octa. John.	7	58	c
4	d	Octa. Innocēt.	8	0	d
5	e	Depo. of Edw	8	3	e
6	f	Twelfe day.	8	6	f
7	g	Felix & Janu.	8	8	g
8	A	Lucian Priest	8	11	h
9	b	Joyce Virgin.	8	14	i
10	c		8	16	k
11	d	Sol in Aquar:	8	18	l
12	e	Atlas.	8	20	m
13	f	Hillarie Bish	8	24	n
14	g	Felicia.	8	26	o
15	A	Maurice:	8	30	p
16	b	Marcell.	8	33	q
17	c	Depo. of Anth.	8	36	r
18	d	Prisca Virgin	8	40	s
19	e	Wolstane bish	8	43	ſ
20	f	Fabian & Seb.	8	46	t
21	g	Agnes Virgin	8	50	u
22	A	Vincent mart.	8	52	v
23	b	Timothe.	8	56	x
24	c	Emerice.	9	0	y
25	d	Conu. of Paule.	9	4	z
26	e	Policarp. mar.	9	6	&
27	f	Chrisost. doct.	9	10	ſt
28	g	Theodor priest	9	1[illegible]	a
29	A	Valerie bishop	9	18	[illegible]
30	b	Bateld queene	9	22	[illegible]
31	c	Saturn & Vict	9	26	d

Dayes.		February.	Length of the day.		☾
1	d	Fast.	9	28	e
2	e	Purifi. of Mary	9	32	f
3	f	Blase. Martyr	9	36	g
4	g	Gilbert confes.	9	40	h
5	A	Agathe virgin	9	44	i
6	b	Dorothe Vir.	9	48	k
7	c	Angalle.	9	52	l
8	d	Sallomon.	9	56	m
9	e	Sol in Pisces.	10	0	n
10	f	Scollastica.	10	4	o
11	g	Sother Bishop	10	8	p
12	A	Eulrase virgin	10	10	q
13	b		10	14	r
14	c	Valentine.	10	18	ſ
15	d		10	22	s
16	e	Julian virgin.	10	29	t
17	f	Germaine.	10	30	v
18	g	Hugh Bishop.	10	34	u
19	A	Simeon.	10	38	x
20	b	Mildred.	10	42	y
21	c	Lxxix. Martirs	10	46	z
22	d	Peters chaires	10	50	&
23	e	Fast.	10	54	ſt
24	f	Mathie Apost.	10	58	a
25	g	Inuent. Poule	11	2	b
26	A	Nestor.	11	7	c
27	b	Alexander.	11	1[illegible]	d
28	c	Augustine.	11	16	e

Dayes.		March.	Length of the daies.		☾	Dayes.		Aprill.	Length of the day.		☽
1	d	Dauid.	11	24	f	1	g	Gilbard.	13	30	k
2	e	Chadde.	11	[illegible]	g	2	A	Marie Egipt.	13	34	l
3	f	Maurice.	11	[illegible]	h	3	b	Richard Bish.	13	38	m
4	g	Adrian.	1[illegible]	36	i	4	c	Ambrose.	13	42	n
5	A	Focas & Euse.	11	40	k	5	d	Uincent.	13	46	o
6	b	Uict. & Uenin.	11	44	l	6	e	Sextus.	13	50	p
7	c	Perpetue.	11	48	n	7	f	Euphemy.	13	52	q
8	d	Depo. of Felix	11	52	[illegible]	8	g	Dionisies.	13	56	r
9	e	Forty martirs	11	56	[illegible]	9	A	Perpetuus.	14	0	ſ
10	f	Agapit.	12	0	[illegible]	10	b	Apolinia.	14	2	s
11	g	Sol in Aries	12	4	q	11	c	Sol in Taurus.	14	4	t
12	A	Gregorie bish	12	8	r	12	d	Sother.	14	8	v
13	b	Theodore.	12	12	s	13	e	Marcus.	14	12	u
14	c	Candide.	12	16	ſ	14	f	Liburtie.	14	16	x
15	d	Longine.	12	20	t	15	g	Osmond.	14	20	y
16	e	Pilla & Ionas	12	24	u	16	A	Isidore.	14	24	z
17	f	Gertude.	12	28	v	17	b	Anisette.	14	28	&
18	g	Edward king.	12	32	x	18	c	Elutherius.	14	32	ꝯ
19	A	Iose. Ma hus.	12	36	y	19	d	Alphege.	14	34	[illegible]
20	b	Cutbart.	12	40	z	20	e	Uictor.	14	38	[illegible]
21	c	Benedict.	12	44	&	21	f	Simion.	14	42	[illegible]
22	d	Afrodose.	12	48	ꝯ	22	g	Sother.	14	46	d
23	e	Theodore.	12	5[illegible]	a	23	A	George Mart	14	[illegible]	e
24	f	Fast.	2	5[illegible]	b	24	b	Wilfride.	14	5[illegible]	f
25	g	Annū of Mari	13	2	c	25	c	Marke Euang	14	[illegible]6	g
26	A	Castor martir	13	9	d	26	d	Clete.	15	[illegible]	h
27	b	Perciany.	13	10	e	27	e	Anastatius.	1[illegible]	[illegible]	i
28	c	Rupert.	13	14	f	28	f	Uitales.	[illegible]	[illegible]	k
29	d	Uictorine.	13	18	g	29	g	Peter of Mi.	[illegible]	[illegible]	l
30	e	Quirine.	13	22	h	[illegible]	a	Dep. of Erken	[illegible]	14	n
31	f	Adeline.	13	2[illegible]	i						

Dayes.		May.	Length of the daies.		☾	Dayes.		Iune.	Length of the day.		☾
1	b	Philip & Iacob.	15	18	a	1	e	Nichomede.	16	24	r
2	c	Athanasius.	15	20	b	2	f	Marcell.	16	25	ſ
3	d	Inu. of ÿ crosse.	15	24	b	3	g	Erasmus.	16	26	s
4	e	Christopher.	15	28	r	4	A	Petrocus.	16	27	t
5	f	Godarde.	15	30	r	5	b	Boneface.	16	28	v
6	g	John Port Lat.	15	32	s	6	c	Helon.	16	28	u
7	A	John of Beuer.	15	34	i	7	d	Paule Bishop	16	39	x
8	b	Aper. of Micha.	15	36	[illegible]	8	e	Trãs. of Edm.	16	30	y
9	c	Trans. of Nic.	15	40	a	9	f	Ianua. confess.	16	30	z
10	d	Gordian.	15	42	d	10	g	Trã of Wolst	16	30	&
11	e	Anthony.	15	44	c	11	A	Barnard Apo.	16	30	st
12	f	Sol in Gemini.	15	46	e	12	b	Sol in Cancer.	16	30	a
13	g	Seruasius.	15	49	z	13	c	Anthonie.	16	30	b
14	A	Boniface mart.	15	52	&	14	d	Basilides.	16	30	c
15	b	Isidore.	15	54	&	15	e	Vite and Mode:	16	29	d
16	c	Discor. Mart.	15	57	a	16	f	Tran of Rich.	16	28	e
17	d	Dunstane.	16	0	b	17	g	Botulphe.	16	28	f
18	e	Bernardine.	16	2	c	18	A	Mar. & Marcel.	16	27	g
19	f	Aquilla.	16	5	d	19	b	Geruasius.	16	27	h
20	g	Dunstone.	16	8	e	20	c	Tran. of Edw.	16	26	i
21	A	Barnardine.	16	10	f	21	d	Wilburge.	16	25	k
22	b	Helena quéene.	16	12	g	22	e	Albane.	16	24	l
23	c	Desideri.	16	14	h	23	f	Fast.	16	23	m
24	d	Serule.	16	15	i	24	g	Iohn Baptist.	16	22	n
25	e	Urbane.	16	16	k	25	A	Amandi.	16	20	o
26	f	Adelme confess.	16	18	l	26	b	Iohn & Paule.	16	19	p
27	g	Bede Priest.	16	19	m	27	c	Crescence.	16	18	q
28	A	Germaine.	16	20	n	28	d	Fast.	16	16	r
29	b	Corone.	16	21	o	29	e	Peter & Paule.	16	15	s
30	c	Felix.	16	22	p	30	f	Com. of Paule.	16	14	ſ
31	d	Petronill.	16	23	q						

Daies.		Iulie.	Length of the daie.		☾	Daye.		August.	Length of the daie.		☾
1	g	Octa of Iohn	16	12	t	1	c	Lamas.	14	46	v
2	A	Visit of Marie	16	1[illegible]	h	2	d	Stephen.	14	42	x
3	b	Trā of Thom	16	8	u	3	e	Inuent. Ste.	14	38	t
4	c	Tran of Mart.	16	5	c	4	f	Iustine.	14	34	x
5	d	CCC virgins.	16	3	p	5	g	Festū Niuis.	14	32	a
6	e	Martalis.	16	2	f	6	A	Trāſfi. of Chr.	14	28	b
7	f	Zenane mart.	16	0	r	7	b	Feast of Iesus	14	24	c
8	g	Depo. of Grem	15	57	x	8	c	Ciriacke.	14	20	d
9	A	Cyrile Bishop.	15	54	l	9	d	Roman mart	14	16	e
10	b	Dog dais begin	15	52	?	10	e	Laurence mar.	14	12	f
11	c	Seuen brethrē	15	49	c	11	f	Cutbert.	14	8	g
12	d	Nabor & Felix.	15	49	d	12	g	Clarie.	14	4	h
13	e	Sol in Leo.	15	46	e	13	A	Hiplit.	14	0	i
14	f	Keuell.	15	42	f	14	b	Sol in Virgo.	14	56	k
15	g	Transl. Suitt	15	40	g	15	c	Assump. Marie	13	52	l
16	A	Trāſ. Oſmōd.	15	37	h	16	d	Roch mart.	13	50	m
17	b	Katherine.	15	34	i	17	e	Octa Laurence	13	46	n
18	c	Arnulfe.	15	30	k	18	f	Lewis.	13	42	o
19	d	Rufian & Iust.	15	28	l	19	g	Barnerd.	13	38	p
20	e	Margaret.	15	24	m	20	A	Dog daies end	13	34	q
21	f	Praxed.	15	20	n	21	b	Priuate.	13	30	r
22	g	Marie Magde.	15	18	o	22	c	Timothe.	13	26	ſ
23	A	Apolinarie.	15	14	p	23	d	Fast.	13	22	s
24	b	Fast.	15	10	q	24	e	Barthol Apost.	13	18	t
25	c	Iames Apostle.	15	8	r	25	f	Lewes King.	13	14	v
26	d	Anne mot. Ma.	15	4	ſ	26	g	Seuerne.	13	10	u
27	e	VII. Sleepers.	15	0	s	27	A	Rufine Martin	13	8	c
28	f	Sampson.	14	58	t	28	b	Augustine bish	13	6	y
29	g	Martha.	14	56	v	29	c	Iohn beheded.	13	2	z
30	A	Abdon & Sen.	14	54	u	30	d	Felix & Audact.	12	58	&
31	b	German.	14	50	c	31	e	Cuthburg	12	54	ꝯ

Daies.		September.	Length of the daie,		☾
1	f	Giles.	12	48	a
2	g	Anthony mar.	12	44	b
3	A	Lupus Bishop.	12	40	c
4	b	Trans. Cuthb.	12	36	d
5	c	Martine,	12	32	e
6	d	Eugenius.	12	28	f
7	e	Nati. Eliz. Reg.	12	24	g
8	f	Natiu. of Mari.	12	20	h
9	g	Gorgonie.	12	16	i
10	A	Siluius Bish.	12	12	k
11	b	Protec, & Hiac.	12	8	l
12	c	Martinian.	12	4	m
13	d	Sol in Libra.	12	0	n
14	e	Holie Crosse.	11	56	o
15	f	Philetus.	11	52	p
16	g	Edith.	11	48	q
17	A	Lambert.	11	44	r
18	b	Vict. and Cor.	11	40	ſ
19	c	Ianuarie mar	11	36	s
20	d	Fast.	11	32	t
21	e	Mathew Apo.	11	28	v
22	f	Mauricius.	11	24	a
23	g	Tecla Virgin	11	20	c
24	A	Andochius.	11	16	y
25	b	Fermine.	11	12	z
26	c	Cipri. & Iust.	11	6	&
27	d	Cosme & Da.	11	2	A
28	e	Exuperius.	10	58	i
29	f	Michael Arch	10	54	l
30	g	Hierome priest	10	[illegible]	[illegible]

Daye.		October.	Length of the daie.		☽
1	a	Remigius.	10	46	[illegible]
2	b	Leodegarie.	10	42	c
3	c	Candide.	10	38	f
4	d	Frances.	10	34	g
5	e	Apoline.	10	30	h
6	f	Faith.	10	26	i
7	g	Martine.	10	22	[illegible]
8	A	Pelagius.	10	18	[illegible]
9	b	Gercon & Vic.	10	14	n
10	c	Nicasius.	10	10	[illegible]
11	d	Edward King.	10	8	[illegible]
12	e	Adorant.	10	4	[illegible]
13	f	Calictes.	10	0	r
14	g	Sol in Scorpio.	9	56	[illegible]
15	A	Wolfran.	9	52	[illegible]
16	b	Mich of ẏ mou:	9	48	s
17	c	Etheldred.	9	44	t
18	d	Luke Euangel.	9	40	v
19	e	Fredeswide	9	36	a
20	f	Austerbert.	9	32	x
21	g	xi. M. Virgins	9	28	y
22	A	Mary Salom.	9	26	z
23	b	Romaine.	9	22	&
24	c	Maglorie.	9	18	A
25	d	Crispine.	9	14	a
26	e	Vrsula.	9	10	b
27	f	Fast.	9	6	c
28	g	Simon & Iude.	9	4	d
29	A	Quintinus.	9	0	e
30	b	German.	8	56	f
31	c	Fast.	8	52	g

Dayes.		Nouember.	Length of the daies.		☽	Dayes.		December.	Length of the day.		☾
1	d	All Saints.	8	50	h	1	f	Elegius.	7	36	l
2	e	All Soule.	8	46	i	2	g	Libane.	7	35	m
3	f	Wenefride.	8	42	k	3	A	Dep. Osmond	7	34	n
4	g	Amantius.	8	40	l	4	b	Barbara.	7	33	o
5	A	Lets Priest.	8	36	m	5	c	Saua.	7	32	p
6	b	Leonard.	8	32	n	6	d	Nicholas bish	7	32	q
7	c	Wilbrode.	8	30	o	7	e	Ambrose.	7	31	r
8	d	Foure crown.	8	26	p	8	f	Conc. of Mary	7	30	ſ
9	e	Theodore.	8	24	q	9	g	Ciprian.	7	30	s
10	f	Benet.	8	20	r	10	A	Eulalia.	7	30	t
11	g	Martine Bish	8	18	s	11	b	Damase.	7	30	v
12	A	Paterne.	8	16	ſ	12	c	Sun in Capric.	7	30	u
13	b	Sunne in Sagit.	8	14	t	13	d	Luce virgin.	7	30	r
14	c	Tran Erken.	8	11	u	14	e	Nicasius bish.	7	30	g
15	d	Machute.	8	8	v	15	f	Valerius.	[illegible]	[illegible]	z
16	e	Dep. Edmond.	8	6	c	16	g	Lazarus con.	7	32	&
17	f	Init. Reg. Eliz.	8	3	[illegible]	17	A	O sapientie.	7	32	ꝯ
18	g	Octa Marie.	8	0	[illegible]	18	b	Gracian.	7	33	a
19	A	Eliza Martir.	7	58	t	19	c	Venesta. Vir.	7	34	b
20	b	Edmond king.	7	55	I	20	d	Fast.	7	35	c
21	c	Present. Ma.	7	52	[illegible]	21	e	Thomas Apo.	[illegible]	36	d
22	d	Cecill virgin.	7	50	[illegible]	22	f	XXX. Martirs	7	37	e
23	e	Clement.	7	47	[illegible]	23	g	Victor.	7	38	f
24	f	Grisogon.	7	45	[illegible]	24	A	Fast.	7	40	g
25	g	Katherine.	7	44	[illegible]	25	b	Christmas day	7	41	h
26	A	Line.	7	42	[illegible]	26	c	Stephen mar.	7	42	i
27	b	Agricola.	7	41	[illegible]	27	d	Iohn Euangel.	7	44	k
28	c	Rufus martir	7	40	[illegible]	28	e	Innocents day	7	45	l
29	d	Satu. E Fast	7	38	[illegible]	29	f	Tra. of Iames	7	46	m
30	e	Andrew Apo.	7	37	[illegible]	30	g	Siluester.	[illegible]	48	n
						31	A			50	o

Aries.	z	o	d	u	m	a	s	i	&	q	f	x	n	v	t	k	ſt	r	g
Aries.	&	p	c	x	n	b	t	w	ſt	r	g	y	o	r	v	l	a	ſ	h
Taurus.	ſt	q	f	y	g	c	v	l	a	ſ	h	z	p	d	u	m	b	s	i
Taurus.	a	r	g	z	p	d	u	m	b	s	i	&	q	e	x	n	c	t	k
Gemini.	v	ſ	h	&	q	e	x	n	c	t	k	ſt	r	ſ	y	o	d	v	l
Gemini.	c	s	i	u	r	f	y	o	d	v	l	a	ſ	g	z	p	e	u	m
Cancer	d	t	k	a	ſ	g	z	p	e	u	m	b	s	h	&	q	f	x	n
Cancer.	e	v	l	b	s	h	&	q	f	x	n	c	t	i	ſt	r	g	y	o
Leo.	f	u	m	c	t	i	w	r	g	y	o	d	v	k	a	ſ	h	z	p
Leo.	g	x	n	d	v	k	a	ſ	h	z	p	e	u	l	v	s	i	&	q
Leo.	h	y	o	c	u	l	b	s	i	&	q	f	x	m	c	t	k	ſt	r
Virgo.	i	z	p	f	x	m	c	t	s	ſt	r	g	y	n	d	v	l	a	ſ
Virgo	k	&	q	g	y	n	d	v	l	a	ſ	h	z	o	e	u	m	b	g
Libra.	l	ſt	r	h	z	o	e	u	m	v	s	i	&	p	f	x	n	c	t
Libra.	m	a	ſ	i	&	p	f	x	n	c	t	k	ſt	q	g	y	o	d	v
Scorpio.	n	b	s	k	ſt	q	g	y	o	d	v	l	a	r	h	z	p	e	u
Scorpio.	o	c	t	l	a	r	h	z	p	e	u	m	b	ſ	i	&	q	f	r
Sagittarius.	p	d	v	m	b	ſ	i	&	q	f	x	n	c	s	k	ſt	r	g	y
Sagittarius.	q	e	u	n	c	s	k	ſt	r	g	y	o	d	t	l	a	ſ	h	z
Sigittarius.	r	f	x	o	d	t	l	a	ſ	h	z	p	e	v	m	b	s	i	&
Capricorne.	ſ	g	y	p	e	v	m	b	s	i	&	q	f	u	n	c	t	k	ſt
Capricorne.	s	h	z	q	f	u	n	c	t	k	ſt	r	g	x	o	d	v	l	a
Aquarius.	t	i	&	r	g	x	o	d	v	l	a	ſ	h	y	p	e	u	m	b
Aquarius.	v	k	ſt	ſ	h	y	p	e	u	m	b	s	i	z	q	f	x	n	c
Pisces.	u	l	a	s	i	z	q	f	x	n	c	t	k	&	r	g	y	o	r
Pisces	x	m	b	t	k	&	r	g	y	o	d	v	l	ſt	ſ	h	z	p	e
Pisces	y	n	c	v	l	ſt	ſ	h	z	o	e	u	m	a	s	i	&	q	f

The vse of the table.

FIrst goe to the Kelender, to the daie of the month which ye desire to know what sign the Moone is in: And in the last cullum of that month vnder the Moone, in the head thereof, directly against the same day, you shall find one of the 24. letters, which you shall beare in memorie, and returne to the Prime of the present yéere, in the head of this Table, descending downe by the cullum of the same prime, vntill yee finde the letter yee beare in memorie, of the Kalender, and directly against this square, or letter in the first cullum yée shall finde named the signe that the Moone then occupieth.

As for example.

The yere 1581. the 12. of June, I desire to know what signe the Moone is in, I goe to the Kalender to that Moneth of June to the 12. day, against which, in the last cullum, vnder the Moone, in the head of the moneth I finde the letter a, which bearing in memorie, I returne to thys Table, to the Prime of this yeare, which I séeke in the table of the moueable feasts, and find to be 5. where I enter the Table, in the head, and in the first cullum, descending downe, vntill I finde (a) against which to the left hand in the first cullum, I finde Scorpio, which sheweth the moone to be in that signe.

THE CONTENTES Of this booke.

The

The eight chapter.

Certaine proofes of the power and action, wholie and freelie beeing in this Stone, to shewe this point Respectiue and in the Needle, by vertue & power receiued of the stone, and not forced, or constrained by any Attractiue in Heauen or Earth.

The ninth chapter.

Of the Variation of the Needle, from the Pole or Axeltree of the Earth, and how it is to be vnderstood.

The tenth chapter.

Of the common Compasses, and of the diuers different sorts and makings of them, with the inconueniences that may grow by them, and the plats made by them.

A Table or Regiment of the sunnes declination, exactly calculated vnto the minute by the true place of the sunne, whose greatest Declination for this age is 23. Degrees 28. minutes, & may serue for 30. yeeres without great errour.

How to vse the sunnes Declination, for knowing the eleuation of the pole.

Three Tables, the first sheweth the coniunctions of the sunne and Moone for 19. yeares, with the Ecclipses of the sunne.

The second Table sheweth the houre and minute of the opposition or full Moones, with the Eclipses of the moone.

The third Table followeth the Kalender, by the which

is alwaies found what signe the Moone is in, with the help of the letters in the Kalender, also by the saide kalender is shewed the houre and minute of the length of the day, for euerie day of the yere, for the eleuation of the Pole. 52. degrees.

A Table to know what Planet rules anie houre either by day or night.

A Table to know the length of the planetarie hour, frō the shortest day and longest night, till the longest day and shortest night.

A Chapter of the longitude and declination of 32. notable fixed starres very necessary for Nauigation, with tables of their shining, and at what point of your Compasse they doo both rise and set: and also Tables for euerie Moneth of the yere, declaring at what houre and minute they be South, running from the first day of the month, to the fifteenth, and from the fifteenth to the last day, and wyll continue these 100. yeeres without much error.

A Table to knowe the rising and setting of these stars, by what point of the Compasse, & how many houres they be aboue our Horizon, the pole being raised 51. or 52 de-

A table of the fixed Starres.
A Table of the true place of the Sunne.
The Table of the Equation of the *Sunne*.
The Chapter of the declination of the Sunne.

A

A Table to know what Planet rules anie houre, either of day or night for euer.

Gouerners of the day.	Sundaie.	Mundaie.	Teusdaie.	Wednesday	Thursday.	Friday.	Saturdaie.	Rulers of the night.
Sol.	1	12	9	o	10	o	11	Iupiter.
Venus.	2	o	10	o	11	1	12	Mars.
Mercurie.	3	o	11	1	12	2	o	Sol.
Luna.	4	1	12	2	o	3	o	Venus.
Saturne.	5	2	o	3	o	4	1	Mercurie.
Iupiter.	6	3	o	4	1	5	2	Luna.
Mars.	7	4	1	5	2	6	3	Saturne.
Sol.	8	5	2	6	3	7	4	Iupiter.
Venus.	9	6	3	7	4	8	5	Mars.
Mercurie.	10	7	4	8	5	o	6	Sol.
Luna.	11	8	5	9	6	10	7	Venus.
Saturne.	12	9	6	10	7	11	8	Mercurie.
Iupiter.	o	10	7	11	8	12	9	Luna.
Mars.	o	11	8	12	9	o	10	Saturne.

The vse of this Table is thus.

VNder the day of your request, seeke the houre that ye desire, thē on the left side right there against shal ye see the Planet that gouernes that houre by daie, & at the right side, the Planet that rules it by night, as thus, On Thursday the third houre of the daie rules ☉. and the 8. houre of the night gouernes ☽. and so of the rest, for it is plaine enough.

A Table to know the length of the planetarie houre, from the shortest day and longest night, till the longest day & shortest night.

M / H	0 H.M.	12 H.M.	24 H.M.	36 H.M.	48 H.M.
7	0. 35	0. 36	0. 37	0. 38	0. 39
8	0. 40	0. 41	0. 42	0. 43	0. 44
9	0. 45	0. 46	0. 47	0. 48	0. 49
10	0. 50	0. 51	0. 52	0. 53	0. 54
11	0. 55	0. 56	0. 57	0. 58	0. 59
12	1. 0	1. 1	1. 2	1. 3	1. 4
13	1. 50	1. 6	1. 7	1. 8	1. 9
14	1. 29	1. 11	1. 12	1. 13	1. 14
15	1. 25	1. 16	1. 17	1. 18	1. 19
16	1. 20	1. 21	1. 22	1. 23	1. 24
17	1. 20	1. 26	1. 27	1. 28	1. 29

The vse is this.

Knowe the length of the day or night, that ye require by the Table proceeding in houres & minutes, and therewith enter this Table, the houre at the side, and the neerest minute at the head, and then discend right against your houre and there in the common angle shall ye find the houre and minute, or minutes onely that the Planet raignes by the houres of the clocks.

As for Example.

The 12. of June the daye is 16. houres, 20. minutes, wherewith I enter this Table as is shewed & in the angle I find 1 houre 22. minutes, which sheweth that a planet that day rules an houre & a quarter, and 7. min. of the clocks. Also for the same night I find it to be but 7. houres 40. minuts, wherewith I enter into this table with 7. at the side, 36. at the head (for that is neerest) and in the common angle I finde but onely 38. minutes, which shewe that a Planet in that night rules but halfe an houre and 8 minutes of the clockes, and so of the rest.

This Chapter is of the longitude, and the Declination of 32. notable fixed Starres, verie necessarie for Nauigation with Tables of their shining, and at what point of your Compasse they do both rise and set: and also tables for euery moneth of the yeare, declaring at what houre and minute they be south, running from the first day of the moneth, to the fifteenth: & from the fifteenth to the last day, and will continue these 100. yeare without much errour.

I Doe thinke it conuenient for diuerse considerations, to shew the longitude and declination of certaine of the most notablest fixed Starres that are neere vnto the Equinoctiall, to the number of 32. of them which are verie necessarie for Nauigation in diuers respectes, as this: If you bee vnto the North partes, where the North Pole is raised more then 50. or 60. degrees, then the North Starre is too high to be obserued or taken with the crosse Staffe (as Master Boorne hath declared in his first Chapter of his Regiment for the Sea) and it may chance so, that in the day the Sun is not to be seene at noone, and then these starres may serue your turne.

If the pole be raised more the 50. or 60. degrees it is to high to be obserued by the crosse staffe.

And further more, they be very good for them that haue occasion to trauaile beyond the Equinoctiall, where the North Pole is vnder the Horizon, in vsing their declination as they doe the Sunnes declination in all pointes (as dooeth appeare in the 7. 8. and 9. Chapter of M. Boornes Regiment.) And moreouer, they bee very necessarie for Sea-faring men to knowe the houres of the night, both by their being vpon the Meridian. and also by their rising and setting, you may knowe the true time of their rising and

These starres will serue beyond the Equinoctiall.

and setting, you may knowe the true time of their rising and setting in euerie Latitude by their declination from the Equinoctiall, whether they decline to the South parts or North partes (as is declared by the declination of the Sunne in the 11. Chapter of M. Boornes Regiment.

And furthermore, by any of these Starres you may trie the Variation of your Compasse by nyght, &c. Nowe shall followe the Table of all these Starres. The first rowe of this Table, containeth the names of the starres: The second the signes, what they be in longitude: The third, the degrees of the signes: The fourth, the minutes belonging thereunto: The fift, the degrees of declination: The sixt, the odde minutes belonging thereunto. The seauenth sheweth towarde what place they decline, by letters, of which S. signifieth the Septentrional, or north declination M. signifieth Meridionall, or south declination, as in the Table doth appeare. The eight doth shewe nothing but the bignesse of the Starres. Now followeth the Table.

The order of the Table following.

A Ta-

The names of the starres.	Signes.	Longit. deg. mi.	Decli. deg. mi.	To what part they decline.	Bignes [illegible]
Whales backe.	Aries.	6. 6	12.11	M	second bignes.
Whales bellie.	Aries.	16. 2	12.20	M	second bignes.
Rams horne.	Aries.	27.42	17.19	S	third bignes.
Rams head.	Taurus.	1. 46	21.16	S	third bignes.
Bulles eie.	Gemini	3. 42	15.42	S	great starres.
Orions left foote.	Gemini	10.12	9. 14	M	a great starre.
Orions left shoulder.	Gemini	11.26	4. 37	S	a starre of the
First Orions girdle.	Gemini	16.22	1. 19	M	second light both
Orios right shulders.	Gemini	23. 6	5. 18	S	a great starre.
Great dogge.	Cancer.	8. 40	15.30	M	a very great star
Lesser dogge.	Cancer.	20.10	5. 4	S	a great star.
Brightest in Hydra.	Leo.	21. 2	4. 47	M	second bignes.
Lions necke.	Leo.	23.16	21.59	S	second bignes.
Lions heart.	Leo.	23.32	14. 3	S	a great star.
Lions backe.	Virgo.	5. 16	22.30	S	second bignes:
Lions taile.	Virgo.	15.32	16.46	S	a great star.
Rauens head.	Libra.	5. 6	19.53	M	of ye third bignes.
Rauens wing.	Libra.	9. 36	17. 8	M	both those.
Virgins spike.	Libra.	17.42	4. 54	M	a great star.
Twixt boots thighs.	Libra.	18. 6	22. 9	S	a great star,
South ballance.	Scorpio	9. 2	13.44	M	second bignes.
North ballance.	Scorpio	13.12	7. 33	M	second bignes.
Scorpions heart.	Sagit.	3. 42	24.47	M	second bignes.
Hercules head.	Sagit.	8. 42	15.20	S	third bignes.
Serpents head.	Sagit.	15.52	14. 7	S	third bignes.
The Eagle.	Capric.	24.51	7. 28	S	second bignes.
Dolphins taile.	Aquar.	8. 27	10. 1	S	third bignes.
Goates taile.	Aquar.	17.22	14.13	M	third bignes.
Water pourers leg	Pisces.	2. 20	15.52	M	third bignes.
Pegasus shoulder.	Pisces.	17. 4	13. 1	S	second bignes.
Pegasus legge.	Pisces.	23.10	26.30	S	second bignes.
Whales tayle.	Pisces.	26.21	21.47	M	third bignes.

The

The vse of this Table is this: when you haue taken the height of any of these starres vpon the Meridian, then looke what declination the Starre hath from the Equinoctiall: If the starre hath North declination, then substract or take awaye the starres declination from the height: If it hath south declination, then adde or put vnto the height, the starres declination, and that will shewe vnto you the height of the Equinoctiall, and then by the height of the Equinoctiall, the height of the pole is knowen, as Master Boorne hath declared in the 7. Chapter of the Regiment for the sea. And now I thinke it conuenient to make a certaine Table, to shewe vnto you at what houre and time any of these stars bee vpon the Meridian, wherby they may the better knowe these starres. I will also shewe vnto you howe long any of these starres doe shine or tarrie aboue the Horizon in this Latitude from the Equinoctiall of London, that is at 51. or 52. degrees. And also at what point of the compasse any of these starres doe rise or set, which will serue this 100. yeares without much errour.

How to vse the stars declination to know the height of the Pole.

A Table to know the rising and setting of these starres by what point of the compasse, & howe many houres they be aboue our Horizon, the pole being raised 51. or 52. degrees.

The Whales backe riseth East and by south, and vnto the southwardes: and shineth 10. houres & better.

The Whales belly (in a manner) as the Whales backe.

The Rams horne riseth East Northeast, and setteth West Northwest, and shineth 15. houres 16. minutes.

The Rammes head riseth East Northeast, and setteth West Northwest, and shineth 16. houres 4. minutes.

The Buls eye riseth neere the East Northeast, and setteth neere the West Northwest, and shineth 15. houres 2. minutes.

The Orions left foote riseth neer ye East and by south and setteth neere the West and by south, and shineth 10. houres

houres and 6.minutes.

The Orions left shoulder riseth East and to the north-wards, and setteth West and to the Northwards, and shi-neth 11.houres 45.minutes.

The first in Orions girdle dooth rise a little to the Southwards of the East, and setteth a little to the south-wards of the West, and shineth 11. houres 46.minutes.

Orions right shoulder riseth East, and unto the North-wards, and setteth West and unto the Northwards; and shineth 13 hour es 12.minutes.

The great dog riseth East southeast, and setteth west southwest, and shineth 9. houres.

The lesser dog riseth East and unto the Northwardes, and setteth West and unto Northwardes, and shineth 13. houres 10. minutes.

The brightest in Hydra riseth East and unto the south-wards, and setteth West and unto southwardes, and shy-neth 11.houres and 7.minutes.

The Lyons necke riseth East Northeast, and to the Northwards, & setteth west Northwest, and to the North-wards, and shineth 16.houres 16.minutes.

The Lyons hart riseth neere the East Northeast, and setteth neere the West Northwest, and shineth 14.houres 50.minutes.

The Lyons backe riseth neere the Northeast and by East, and setteth neere the Northwest and by weast, and shineth 16.houres 26.minutes.

The Lyons taile riseth neere the East Northeast, and setteth neere the West Northwest, and shineth 15.houres 12.minutes.

The Rauens head riseth neere the East southeast, and setteth neere the West southwest, and shineth 8. houres 12.minutes.

The Rauens wing riseth neere the East southeast, and setteth neere the west southwest, and shineth 8. houres 50.minutes.

The

The virgins spike riseth East and to the southwards, and setteth West and to the southwards, and shineth 11. houres 4. minutes.

Betwéen boots thighs, riseth néere the Northeast and by East, and setteth neere the Northwest, and by West, and shineth 16. houres 20. minutes.

The South ballance riseth neere the East southeast, and setteth neere the West south west: and shineth 9. hours 36. minutes.

The North ballance riseth neere the East and by south and setteth neere the West and by south, and shineth 10 houres 38. minutes.

The Scorpions heart riseth neere the southeast and by east, and setteth neere the southwest and by West, and shineth 7. houres. 5 minutes.

Hercules head riseth neere the East Northeast, and setteth néere the West Northwest, and shineth 14. houres, 56 minutes.

The Serpents head riseth néere the East Northeast, and setteth neere the West Northwest, , and shineth 14. houres 40. minutes,

The Eagle riseth neere by East and by North, and setteth neere the West and by North, and shineth 13. houres 24. minutes.

The Dolphins taile riseth East and by North, and setteth West and by North, and shineth 15. houres 57. minutes.

The 11 Chapter of M. Boordes Regiment for the Sea, will shewe howe long any of these starres will shine in all places.

The Goates taile riseth neere the East southeast, and setteth West southwest, and shineth 9. houres 20. minutes.

The Water powrers leg riseth neere the East southeast, and setteth West southwest, and shineth 8. houres, 54. minutes.

Pegasus shoulders riseth neere the East Northeast, and setteth neere the West Northwest, and shineth 14. houres 32. minutes.

Pegasus

Pegasus legge riseth neere Northeast, and setteth neere Northwest, and shineth 17. houres. 6 minutes.

The Whales taile riseth East Southeast, and setteth West Southwest, and shineth 7. houres 48. minutes.

Furthermore, if you desire to knowe the time of any of these starres beeing aboue the Horizon in all Latitudes, then repaire to the eleuenth Chapter of Maister Boornes Regement for the sea, so you shall knowe it there by their declination: euen by the same order that you knowe the Sunnes beeing aboue the Horizon, by the Sunnes declination.

A Table of the fixed Starres.

	These Starres being South from the first day of Ianu. vnto the 15				Ianu. from the 15 to the last			Febru. fro the 5 vnto the 15			Febru. fro the 15 to the last	
1	Whales backe.	5. 29	E	1	4.20	DA	1	3.20	DA	1	2.20	DA
2	Whales bellie.	5. 54	E	2	4.54	DA	2	3.54	DA	2	2.54	DA
3	Rammes horne.	6. 28	E	3	5.28	E	3	4.28	DA	3	3.28	DA
4	Rammes head.	6. 45	E	4	5.45	E	4	4.44	DA	4	3.45	DA
5	Buls eie.	8. 52	E	5	7.52	E	5	5.52	E	5	5.52	DA
6	Orions left foote.	9. 23	E	6	8.23	E	6	7.23	E	6	5.23	E
7	Orions left shulder.	9. 28	E	7	8.28	E	7	7.28	E	7	5.28	E
8	First Orions girdle	9. 50	E	8	8.50	E	8	7.50	E	8	6 50	E
9	Orions right shulder	10.12	E	9	9.12	E	9	8 12	E	9	7 12	E
10	Great dogge.	11. 4	E	10	10.4	E	10	9. 4	E	10	8. 4	E
11	Lesser dogge.	12. 0		11	11.0	E	11	10.0	E	11	9. 0	E
12	Brightest in hydry	12. 4	M	12	11.4	E	12	10.4	E	12	9. 4	E
13	Lions necke.	2. 12	M	13	1.12	M	13	12.12	M	13	11.12	E
14	Lions heart.	2. 13	M	14	1.13	M	14	12.13	M	14	11.13	E
15	Lions backe.	3. 0	M	15	2. 0	M	15	1. 0	M	15	12.0	
16	Lions tayle.	3. 42	M	16	2.42	M	16	1.42	M	16	1 42	M
17	Rauens head.	5. 2	M	17	4. 2	M	17	3. 2	M	17	2. 2	M
18	Rauens wing.	5. 19	M	18	4.19	M	18	3.19	M	18	2.19	M
19	Virgins spike.	5. 51	M	19	4.51	M	19	3.51	M	19	2.51	M
20	Twixt boot thighs.	5. 56	M	20	4.56	M	20	3.56	M	20	2.56	M
21	South Balance.	7. 16	M	21	5.16	M	21	5.16	M	21	4.56	M
22	North Balance.	7. 33	MD	22	6.33	M	22	5.53	M	22	4.33	M
23	Scorpions heart.	8. 54	MD	23	7.54	MD	23	6.54	M	23	5.54	M
24	Hercules head.	9. 14	MD	24	8.14	MD	24	7.14	MD	24	6.14	M
25	Serpentes head.	9. 41	MD	25	8.41	MD	25	7 41	MD	25	5.41	M
26	The Eagle.	12.19	DA	26	11.19	MD	26	10.19	MD	26	9.19	MD
27	Dolphins tayle.	1. 12	DA	27	12.12	DA	27	11.12	MD	27	10.12	MD
28	Goates tayle.	1. 48	DA	28	12.48	DA	28	11.48	MD	28	10.48	MD
29	Water powrers leg.	2. 48	DA	29	1.48	DA	29	12.48	DA	29	11 48	MD
30	Pegasus shoulder.	3. 47	DA	30	2.47	DA	30	1.47	DA	30	12.47	DA
31	Pegasus leg.	4. 12	DA	31	3.12	DA	31	2.12	DA	31	1.12	DA
32	Whales tayle.	4. 24	DA	32	3.24	DA	32	2.24	DA	32	1.24	DA

March.

A Table of the fixed Starres.

March from the first to the 15.		March fro the 15. to the last.		Aprill from the first to the 15.		Aprill from the 15 to the last.		May from the first to the 15	
1	1. 20 DA	1	11.20 DA	1	11.20 MD	1	10.20 MD	1	9.20 MD
2	1. 54 DA	2	12.54 DA	2	11.54 MD	2	10.54 MD	2	9.54 MD
3	2. 28 DA	3	1.28 DA	3	12.28 DA	3	11.28 MD	3	10.28 MD
4	2. 45 DA	4	1.45 DA	4	12.45 DA	4	11.45 MD	4	10.45 MD
5	4. 52 DA	5	3.52 DA	5	2.52 DA	5	1,52 DA	5	12.52 DA
6	5. 23 DA	6	4.23 DA	6	3.23 DA	6	2,23 DA	6	1.23 DA
7	5. 28 DA	7	4.28 DA	7	3.28 DA	7	2.28 DA	7	1.28 DA
8	5. 50 DA	8	4.50 DA	8	3.50 DA	8	2.50 DA	8	1.50 DA
9	6. 12 E	9	5.12 DA	9	4.12 DA	9	3.12 DA	9	2.12 DA
10	7. 4 E	10	6. 4 DA	10	5. 4 DA	10	4. 4 DA	10	3. 4 DA
11	8. 0 E	11	7. 0 E	11	6. 0 DA	11	5. 0 DA	11	4. 0 DA
12	8. 4 E	12	7. 4 E	12	6. 4 DA	12	5. 4 DA	12	4. 4 DA
13	10.12 E	13	9.12 E	13	8 12 E	13	7.12 DA	13	6.12 DA
14	10.13 E	14	9.13 E	14	8.13 E	14	7.13 DA	14	6.13 DA
15	11. 0 E	15	10. 0 E	15	9. 0 E	15	8. 0 E	15	7. 0 DA
16	11.42 E	16	10.42 E	16	9.42 E	16	8.42 E	16	7.42 DA
17	1. 2 M	17	12. 2 M	17	11.2 E	17	10.2 E	17	9. 2 E
18	1. 19 M	18	12.19 M	18	11.19 E	18	10.19 E	18	9.19 E
19	1. 51 M	19	12.51 M	19	11.51 E	19	10.51 E	19	9.51 E
20	1. 56 M	20	12.56 M	20	11.56 E	20	10.56 E	20	9.56 E
21	3. 16 M	21	2.16 M	21	1.16 M	21	12.16 M	21	11.16 E
22	3. 33 M	22	2.33 M	22	1.33 M	22	12.33 M	22	11.33 E
23	4. 54 M	23	3.54 M	23	2.54 M	23	1.54 M	23	12.54 M
24	5. 14 M	24	4.14 M	24	3.14 M	24	2.14 M	24	1.14 M
25	5. 41 M	25	4.41 M	25	3.41 M	25	1.41 M	25	3.41 M
26	8. 19 DM	26	7.19 MD	26	5,19 MD	26	5.19 MD	26	4.19 M
27	9. 12 DM	27	8.12 MD	27	7.12 MD	27	9,12 MD	27	5.12 MD
28	9. 48 DM	28	8.48 MD	28	7.48 MD	28	7.48 MD	28	5.48 MD
29	10.48 DM	29	9.48 MD	29	8.48 MD	29	7.48 MD	29	6 48 MD
30	11.47 DM	30	10.47 MD	30	9.47 MD	30	8.47 MD	30	7.47 MD
31	12.12 DA	31	11.12 MD	31	10.12 MD	31	9.12 MD	31	8.12 MD
32	12.24 DA	32	11.24 MD	32	10.24 MD	32	9.24 MD	32	3.24 MD

A Table of the fixed Starres.

May from the 15. to the last.			Iune from the first to the 15.			Iune from the 15 to the last			Iuly from the first to the 15.			Iuly from the 15 to the last.		
1	8.20	MD	1	7.20	MD	1	[illegible].20	ML	1	5.20	MD	1	4.20	M
2	8.54	MD	2	7.54	MD	2	5.54	ML	2	5 54	MD	2	4.54	MD
3	9.28	MD	3	8.28	ML	3	7.28	MD	3	6 28	MD	3	5.28	MD
4	9.45	MD	4	8.45	MD	4	7.45	MD	4	6.45	MD	4	5.45	MD
5	11.52	MD	5	10.52	MD	5	9.52	ML	5	8.52	MD	5	7.52	MD
6	12.23	DA	6	11.23	MD	6	10.23	MD	6	9.23	MD	6	8.23	MD
7	12.28	DA	7	11.28	MD	7	10.28	ML	7	9.28	MD	7	8.28	MD
8	12.50	DA	8	11.50	MD	8	10.50	MD	8	9.50	MD	8	8.50	MD
9	1.12	DA	9	12.12	DA	9	11.12	MD	9	10.12	MD	9	9.12	MD
10	2. 4	DA	10	1. 4	D-	10	12.4	DA	10	11.4	MD	10	10.4	MD
11	3. 0	DA	11	2. 0	DA	11	1. 0	DA	11	12.0		11	11.0	MD
12	3. 4	DA	12	2. 4	DA	12	1. 4	DA	12	12.4	DA	12	11.4	MD
13	5.12	DA	13	4.12	DA	13	3.12	DA	13	2.12	DA	13	1.12	DA
14	5.13	DA	14	4.13	DA	14	3.13	DA	14	2.13	DA	14	1.13	DA
15	6. 0	DA	15	5. 0	DA	15	4. 0	DA	15	3. 0	DA	15	2. 0	DA
16	6.42	DA	16	5.42	DA	16	4.42	DA	16	3 42	DA	16	2.42	DA
17	8. 2	DA	17	7. 2	DA	17	6.2	DA	17	5. 2	DA	17	4. 2	DA
18	8.19	DA	18	7.19	DA	18	6.19	DA	18	5.19	DA	18	4.19	DA
19	8.51	DA	19	7.51	DA	19	6.51	DA	19	5.51	DA	19	4.51	DA
20	8.56	DA	20	7.56	DA	20	5.56	DA	20	5.56	DA	20	4.56	DA
21	10.16	E	21	9.16	DA	21	8.16	DA	21	7.16	DA	21	6.16	DA
22	10.33	E	22	9.33	DA	22	8.33	DA	22	7.33	DA	22	6.33	DA
23	11.54	E	23	10.54	E	23	9.54	DA	23	8.54	DA	23	7.54	DA
24	12.14	M	24	11.14	E	24	10.14	F	24	9.14	E	24	8.14	E
25	12.41	M	25	21.41	E	25	10.41	E	25	9.41	E	25	8.41	E
26	3.19	M	26	2.19	M	26	1.19	E	26	12.19	M	26	11.19	E
27	4.12	MD	27	3.12	M	27	2.12	M	27	1.12	M	27	12.12	E
28	4.48	MD	28	3.48	M	28	2.48	M	28	2.48	M	28	12.48	M
	5.48	MD	29	4.48	MD	29	3.48	M	29	2.48	M	19	1 48	M
	6.47	MD	30	5.47	MD	30	4. 7	MD	30	3.47	M	30	2.47	M
31	7.12	MD	31	5.12	MD	31	5.12	MD	31	4.12	MD	31	3.12	M
32	7.24	MD	32	6.24	MD	32	5.24	MD	32	2.24	MD	32	3.24	M

August frō the first to the 15			Augu. frō the 15. to the last			Septem. frō the first to the 15.			Septe. frō the 15. to the last			Decē frō the first to the 15		
1	3.20	M	1	2.20	M	1	1.20	M	1	12.20	M	1	11.20	E
2	3.54	M	2	2.54	M	2	1.54	M	2	12.54	M	2	11.54	E
3	4.28	M	3	3.28	M	3	2.28	M	3	1.28	M	3	12.28	M
4	3.45	MD	4	3.45	M	4	2.45	M	4	1.45	M	4	12.45	M
5	5.52	MD	5	5.52	ML	5	4.52	M	5	3.52	M	5	2.52	M
6	7.23	MD	6	5.23	ML	6	5.23	M	6	4.23	M	6	3.23	M
7	7.28	MD	7	6.28	ML	7	5.28	M	7	4.28	M	7	3.28	M
8	7.50	MD	8	6.50	MD	8	5.50	MD	8	4.50	M	8	3.50	M
9	8.12	MD	9	7.12	MD	9	6.12	MD	9	5.12	M	9	4.12	M
10	9. 4	MD	10	8. 4	MD	10	7. 4	MD	10	5. 4	MD	10	5. 4	M
11	10.0	MD	11	9. 0	MD	11	8. 0	MD	11	7. 0	MD	11	6. 0	M
12	10.4	MD	12	9. 4	MD	12	8. 4	MD	12	7. 4	MD	12	6. 4	M
13	12.12	DA	13	11.12	MD	13	10.12	MD	13	9.12	MD	13	8.12	MD
14	12.13	DA	14	11.13	ML	14	10.13	MD	14	9.13	MD	14	8.13	MD
15	1. 0	DA	15	12. 0		15	11. 0	MD	15	10.0	MD	15	9. 0	MD
16	1.42	DA	16	12.42	DA	16	11.42	MD	16	10.42	MD	16	9.42	MD
17	3. 2	DA	17	2. 2	DA	17	1. 2	DA	17	12.2	DA	17	11.2	MD
18	3.19	DA	18	2.19	DA	18	1.19	DA	18	12.19	DA	18	11.19	MD
19	3.51	DA	19	2.51	DA	19	1.51	DA	19	12.51	DA	19	11.51	MD
20	3.56	DA	20	2.56	DA	20	1.56	DA	20	12.56	DA	20	11.56	MD
21	5.16	DA	21	4.16	DA	21	3.16	DA	21	2.16	DA	21	1.16	DA
22	5.33	DA	22	4.33	DA	22	3.33	DA	22	2.33	DA	22	1.33	DA
23	6.54	DA	23	5.54	DA	23	4.54	DA	23	3.54	DA	23	2.54	DA
24	7.14	DA	24	6.14	DA	24	5.14	DA	24	4.14	DA	24	3.14	DA
25	7.41	DA	25	6.41	DA	25	5.41	DA	25	4.41	DA	25	3.41	DA
26	10.19	E	26	9.19	E	26	8.19	E	26	7.19	E	26	6.19	E
27	11.12	E	27	10.12	E	27	9.12	E	27	8.12	E	27	7.12	E
28	11.48	E	28	10.48	E	28	9.48	E	28	8.48	E	28	7.48	E
29	12.48	M	29	11.48	E	29	10.48	E	29	9.48	E	29	8.48	E
30	1.47	M	30	12.47	E	30	11.47	M	30	10.47	E	30	9.47	E
31	2.12	M	31	1.12	M	31	12.12	M	31	11.12	E	31	10.12	E
32	2.24	M	32	1.24	M	32	12.24	M	32	11.24	E	32	10.24	E

A Table of the fixed Starres.

Octo. fro the 15 to the last			Nouem. fro the first to the 15.			Noue. fro the 15 to the last			Decem. fro the first to the 15.			Dece. fro the 15 to the last		
1	10.20	E	1	9.20	E	1	8.20	[illegible]	1	7.20	E	1	5.20	E
2	14.54	E	2	9.54	E	2	8.54	E	2	7.54	E	2	6.54	E
3	11.28	E	3	10.28	E	3	9.28	E	3	8.28	E	3	7.28	E
4	11.45	E	4	10.45	E	4	9.45	E	4	8.45	E	4	7.45	E
5	1. 52	M	5	12.52	M	5	11.52	E	5	10.52	E	5	9.52	E
6	2. 23	M	6	1.23	M	6	12.23	M	6	11.23	E	6	10.23	E
7	2. 28	M	7	1.28	M	7	12.28	M	7	11.28	E	7	10.28	E
8	2. 50	M	8	1.50	M	8	12.50	M	8	11.50	E	8	10.50	E
9	3. 12	M	9	2.12	M	9	1.12	M	9	12.12	M	9	11.12	E
10	4. 4	M	10	3. 4	M	10	2. 4	M	10	1. 4	M	10	12.4	M
11	5. 0	M	11	4. 0	M	11	3. 0	M	11	2. 0	M	11	1. 0	M
12	5. 4	M	12	4. 4	M	12	3. 4	M	12	2. 4	M	12	1. 4	M
13	7. 12	MD	13	6.12	M	13	5.12	M	13	4.12	M	13	2.12	M
14	7. 13	MD	14	5.13	M	14	5.13	M	14	4.13	M	14	2.13	M
15	8. 0	MD	15	7. 0	M	15	6. 0	M	15	4. 0	M	15	4. 0	M
16	8. 42	MD	16	7.42	MD	16	6.42	M	16	5.42	M	16	4.42	M
17	10. 2	MD	17	9. 2	MD	17	8. 2	MD	17	7. 2	M	17	6. 2	M
18	10.19	MD	18	9.19	MD	18	8.19	MD	18	7. 19	M	18	5.19	M
19	10.51	MD	19	9.51	MD	19	8.51	MD	19	7.51	MD	19	5.51	M
20	10.56	MD	20	9.56	MD	20	8.56	MD	20	7.56	MD	20	6 56	M
21	12.16	DA	21	11.16	MD	21	10 19	MD	21	9.16	MD	21	8.16	MD
22	12.33	DA	22	11.33	MD	22	10.33	MD	22	9.33	MD	22	8.33	MD
23	1. 54	DA	23	12.54	DA	23	11.54	MD	23	10 54	MD	23	5.54	MD
24	2. 14	DA	24	1.14	DA	24	12.14	DA	24	11.14	MO	24	10.14	MD
25	2. 41	DA	25	1.41	DA	25	12.41	DA	25	11.41	MD	25	10.41	MD
26	5. 19	DA	26	4.19	DA	26	3.19	DA	26	2.19	DA	26	10.19	DA
27	6. 12	E	27	5.12	E	27	4 12	E	27	3.12	DA	27	2.12	DA
28	5. 48	E	28	5.48	E	28	4.48	E	28	3.48	DA	28	2.48	DA
29	7. 48	E	29	6.48	E	29	5.48	E	29	4.48	E	29	3.48	DA
30	8. 47	E	30	7.47	E	30	6.47	E	30	5 47	E	30	4.47	E
31	9. 12	E	31	3.12	E	31	7.12	E	31	5.12	E	31	5.12	E
32	9. 24	E	32	8 24	F	32	7.24	M	32	5.24	E	32	5.24	E

Now

NOW this Table serueth for euery moneth in the yeare (being exactly calculated) their time of their being South, or touching your Meridian, (or as some tearme it) Noonstead, seruing very well the Seamen to take the height of them, with their Instruments vpon the sea, referring it vnto the Table of declination that goeth before: The first is the houres, the second the minutes, the third be the letters that shew you whether they be south by day or by night, in the euening or morning, in the forenoone or afternoone, of the which the letter E. doth signifie euening, ẏ letter M. signifieth morning, the letters DM. signifieth day in the morning, & the letter DA. signifieth day in the afternoone (as I said before) the very hour and minute being South. Nowe you see that I haue put to their being south in the day, as well as in the night, to the intent to know the houre of the night, aswel by their setting, as allo by our compasse, by bringing your 32. points into 24. houres: And in like maner (as M. Boorne hath shewed in ẏ 4. chapter of his Regiment for the Sea) by shining of ẏ Moon to deuide the shining into equal parts, then those parts being equally deuided with the houre and minutes, & the time before their being south put together ẏ halfe that shineth & that, sheweth the iust rising of the stars, & the other time of their shining after the height beeing south, sheweth their setting: Now you, séeing the table runneth frō the first side of euery month, to the 15. from the 15. to the last day, must consider (if you will know ẏ exact time betweene the 1. day and the 15. daie, and betwixt the 25. day, and the last) to do this, looke how many daies of the month is past, either from the first daye or fifteenth day, and pul foure minutes from that number: for so manie daies as is past, for euery day that shall shewe you the true time of their being South, that known, you shall do (as is aforesaid) for their rising and setting.

A Table of the true place of the Sunne.

Months	Ianu.		Februar.		March.		Aprill.		Maie.		Iune.	
Signs	Capric.		Aquarius		Pisces.		Aries.		Taurus.		Gemini.	
Daies	G	M	G	M	G	M	G	M	G	M	G	M
1	20	22	21	53	20	55	21	24	20	21	19	55
2	21	24	22	54	21	55	22	22	21	18	20	52
3	22	25	23	54	22	54	23	21	22	16	21	49
4	23	26	24	55	23	54	24	19	23	11	22	46
5	24	27	25	55	24	53	25	17	24	13	23	43
6	25	28	26	56	25	53	26	16	35	8	24	40
7	26	30	27	56	26	52	27	14	26	5	25	37
8	27	31	28	56	27	52	28	12	27	3	26	34
9	28	32	29	57	28	51	29	10	38	0	27	31
10	29	33	☉♓	57	29	50	☉♈	8	28	58	28	28
11	☉♒	35	1	57	☉♈	49	1	5	29	55	29	25
12	1	36	2	58	1	48	2	4	☉♊	52	☉♋	22
13	2	37	3	58	2	47	3	2	1	50	1	19
14	3	38	4	58	3	46	4	0	2	47	2	16
15	4	39	5	58	4	45	5	58	3	44	3	13
16	5	40	6	58	5	44	6	56	4	41	4	10
17	6	41	7	58	6	43	7	54	5	38	5	7
18	7	42	8	58	7	42	8	52	5	36	6	4
19	8	43	9	58	8	31	9	49	7	33	7	1
20	9	44	10	58	9	39	10	47	8	30	8	58
21	10	55	11	58	10	38	11	45	9	27	9	55
22	11	46	12	58	11	37	12	43	10	24	10	52
23	12	47	13	57	12	36	13	40	11	21	11	49
24	13	48	14	47	13	34	14	38	13	18	12	46
25	14	48	15	57	14	33	15	36	14	15	13	43
26	15	49	16	56	15	32	16	33	15	12	14	40
27	16	50	17	56	16	30	17	31	16	10	25	37
28	17	51	18	56	17	29	18	28	17	7	16	34
29	18	51	19	56	18	28	19	26	18	4	17	31
30	19	52			19	27		23	18	1		29
31	20	52			20	25			[illegible]	58		

A Table of the true place of Sunne.

Months	Iulie.		August.		Septēber		Octob.		Nouem.		Decem.	
Signes	Cancer		Leo.		Virgo.		Libra.		Scorpio.		Sagitta	
Daies	G	M	G	M	G	M	G	M	G	M	G	M
1	18	26	18	2	18	4	17	39	18	49	19	24
2	19	23	19	0	19	2	18	39	19	50	20	26
3	20	20	19	58	20	1	19	38	20	51	21	27
4	21	17	20	55	21	0	20	38	21	52	22	29
5	22	14	21	53	21	58	21	38	22	53	23	30
6	23	11	22	51	22	57	22	38	23	54	24	31
7	24	8	23	48	23	56	23	38	24	55	25	33
8	25	5	24	46	24	55	24	38	25	56	26	34
9	26	2	25	44	25	54	25	39	26	57	27	36
10	27	0	26	42	26	53	26	39	27	58	28	37
11	7	57	27	40	27	52	27	39	28	59	29	39
12	28	54	28	38	28	51	28	39	☉♐	0	☉♑	40
13	29	51	29	36	29	50	29	39	1	1	1	42
14	☉♌	48	☉♍	34	☉♎	49	☉♏	39	2	3	2	43
15	1	46	1	32	1	48	1	40	3	4	3	45
16	2	43	2	30	2	47	2	40	4	5	4	46
17	3	40	2	28	3	46	3	40	5	6	5	48
18	4	38	4	26	4	45	4	41	6	8	6	49
19	5	35	5	24	5	44	5	41	7	9	7	51
20	6	32	6	22	6	44	5	42	8	10	8	52
21	7	30	7	21	7	43	7	42	9	11	9	54
22	8	27	8	19	8	42	8	43	10	12	10	55
23	9	25	9	17	9	42	9	43	11	13	11	57
24	10	22	10	16	10	41	10	44	12	14	12	58
25	11	20	11	14	11	41	11	45	13	15	13	59
26	12	17	12	13	12	41	12	45	14	16	15	1
27	13	15	13	11	13	40	13	46	15	18	16	2
28	14	12	14	10	14	40	14	47	16	19	17	3
29	15	10	15	8	15	39	15	47	17	20	18	5
30	16	7	16	7	16		16	48	18	22	19	6
31	17	5	17	5			17	49		23	20	7

The table of the Equation of the Sunne.

The yeres of our Lord.	The equatiō to be added.		the yere of, &c,	the equation, &c.		the yeres of, &c.	the equation, &c.		the yeres of, &c.	the equation, &c.	
	G	M		G	M		G	M		G	M
1545	1	0	1581	1	16	1617	1	32	1653	1	48
1546		45	1582	1	1	1618	1	17	1654	1	33
1547		30	1583		46	1619	1	2	1655	1	18
1548		15	1584		32	1620		47	1656	1	3
1549	1	2	1585	1	18	1621	1	33	1657	1	49
1550		47	1586	1	3	1622	1	18	1658	1	34
1551		32	1587		48	1623	1	3	1659	1	19
1552		18	1588		33	1624		49	1660	1	4
1553	1	4	1589	1	19	1625	1	35	1661	1	51
1554		49	1590	1	4	1626	1	20	1662	1	36
1555		34	1591		49	1627	1	25	1663	1	21
1556		19	1592		35	1628		51	1664	1	7
1557	1	5	1593	1	21	1629	1	37	1665	1	53
1558		50	1594	1	6	1630	1	22	1666	1	38
1559		35	1595		51	1631	1	7	1667	1	23
1560		21	1596		37	1632		53	1668	1	9
1561	1	7	1597	1	23	1633	1	38	1669	1	55
1562		52	1598	1	8	1634	1	23	1670	1	40
1563		37	1599		53	1635	1	8	1671	1	25
1564		23	1600		39	1636		54	1672	1	10
1565	1	9	1601	1	25	1637	1	40	1673	1	56
1566		54	1602	1	10	1638	1	5	1674	1	41
1567		39	1603		55	1639	1	10	1675	1	26
1568		25	1604		40	1640		56	1676	1	12
1569	1	11	1605	1	26	1641	1	42	1677	1	58
1570		56	1606	1	11	1642	1	27	1678	1	33
1571		41	1607		56	1643	1	12	1679	1	28
1572		26	1608		32	1644		8	1680	1	13
1573	1	12	1609	1	28	1645	1	44	1681	R2	☉
1574		57	1610	1	13	1646	1	29	1682	1	45
1575		42	1611		58	1647	1	14	1683	1	30
1576		28	1612		44	1648	1	0	1684	1	15
1577	1	14	1613	1	30	1649	1	46	1685	1	2
1578		99	1614	1	15	1650	1	31	1686	1	4
1579		44	1615	1	10	1651	1	16	1681	1	32
1580		29	1616		46	1652	1	2	1688	1	8

This Table of the Equation of the Sunne, serueth from the yeare 1545. where it hath his rote or beginning, vntil 1680. and in the yeare of 1681. it shall returne to the roote, adding therunto one degrée more. As for example: In the yere of 1681. adde one degrée vpon the other degree that the roote hath, and so shal the yere of 1681. haue two degrées of equation, and the yeare of 1682. shall haue one degrée and 45'. Minutes, which is to adde one degrée vpon 45. minutes. that had the yeare 1546. &c. And hauing passed ouer 136. yeares, you shall returne to the roote, adding 2. degrées.

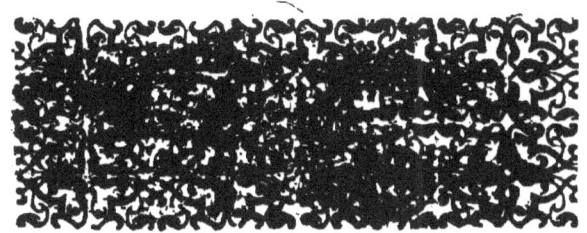

The

Signes.	♈	♎	♉	♏	♊	♐	Signes.
G	G	M	G	M	G	M	G
0	0		11	30	20	12	30
1	0	24	11	51	20	25	29
2	0	48	12	12	20	37	28
3	1	12	12	33	20	49	27
4	1	46	12	53	21	0	26
5	2	0	13	13	21	11	25
6	2	23	13	33	21	22	24
7	2	47	13	53	21	32	23
8	3	11	14	13	21	42	22
9	3	35	14	32	21	51	21
10	3	58	14	51	22	0	20
11	4	22	15	10	22	9	19
12	4	45	15	28	22	17	18
13	5	9	15	47	22	25	17
14	5	32	16	5	22	32	16
15	5	55	16	23	22	39	15
16	6	19	16	40	22	46	14
17	6	42	16	57	22	52	13
18	7	5	17	14	23	57	12
19	7	28	17	31	23	3	11
20	7	50	17	47	23	8	10
21	8	13	18	3	23	12	9
22	8	35	18	19	23	15	8
23	8	58	18	34	23	19	7
24	9	20	18	49	23	22	6
25	9	42	19	4	23	24	5
25	10	4	19	18	23	26	4
27	10	26	19	32	23	28	3
28	10	47	19	46	23	29	2
29	11	9	19	59	23	30	1
30	11	30	20	12	23	30	0
Signes.	♓	♍	♒	♌	♑	♋	Signes.

The Chapter of the Declination of the Sunne.

THE Declination of the Sunne, is the arke of the greater circle, which passeth by the poles of the world, included betwéen the Equinoctiall and the Zodiack. And heere is to bee noted, that whatsoeuer foure pointes or prickes which are equallie distant from the point of the Equinoxis (which are the beginning of Aries and Libra) shall haue equall Declinations.

Whereof it followeth, that the foure quarters of the Zodiacke haue equall declinations. And to auoide prolixity I haue added hereunto a table of the declinations of onely one quarter of the Zodiack, so that all hauing one selfe same maner of Declinations, it may serue for all, & the order of it is this. The signes whose Declination increaseth are in the head or front of the table, and yͤ degrées of these signes descend by the left side therof, & the signes whose declination decreaseth, are in yͤ foot of the table: and the degrees of these signes, rise by the right side of the same. The disposition of the table being vnderstood, then to knowe what declination the sunne hath in euerie degrée of yͤ Zodiack, you ought to know the true place of the sunne, for the day of the declinatiō which you desire to know, and the signe which the sun shall bee found in that day, shal you séeke in yͤ front or foot of the table. And if it be in the front, you shall seeke the number of the degrées on yͤ left side, and if it shalbée at the foot of the table, you shal séeke it on the right side. Then aboue or vnder the signe in the front of yͤ degree of the said signe, you shall find two numbers, wherof yͤ first is of degrées, & the second of minutes: and those degrees and minutes of declination, the Sunne hath that day. And this is vnderstood without hauing respect to yͤ odds odde minuts aboue the degrée, which the true place of the Sunne hath.

And if you desire to verifie this more precisely, note the Declination of that degrée, and of the degrée following: and take the lesse from the more, and that which remayneth, shalbe the difference of the declination from the one degrée to the other: of which difference ye shal take a part proportionallie, as are the minutes of the place of the sun unto 60. And this part of minutes muste bee added to the first declination of it, and be lesse then the second, or must be taken from it, if it shall be greater, and then that riseth thereof shall be the precise declination for that signe, degrée, and minute. As for example: In the yeare 1546. the tenth day of September, the Sun shall be in 26. G. 38. M. of Virgo, & the 25. G precise, shal correspond. 1. G. 36. M. of declination. And to verifie the declination that commeth to 38 minuts, which is more of the 26. G. you must marke the difference that is from the declination of 26. G (which is one G. 36. M.) to the declination of the 27. G. which is one G. 12. M. The difference is 24. M. Of these you must take such part proportionally as the 38. minuts beareth unto 60. which are almost two terces of a degree: Then the two terces of 24. or 16. which must bee taken from one degrée 36. minutes, which corresponde to the 26. G. of Virgo, because the declinations goe decreasing, and remaineth 1. G, 20. M. and if the declinatiōs increase, you must adde thereunto, as you take away when they decrease.

Another example for this yeare of 1561.

Example for the yéere 1561. the 20. of April, I find the true place of the Sunne at noon, in 9 degrées 54. minutes of Taurus, then in the table of the signes before, I séek for 9. degrées of Taurus, to which doth answere for the declination 14. degrées 32. minuts, and to the next degrée following doth answere 14. degrées 51. minutes, then take the

the lesser out of the more, so resteth 19. minutes. Then forme a rule of thrée, and say: if 60. minutes giue 54. minutes, (which 54. minutes doeth rest before of the 9. degrees of Taurus) how many doth 19. minutes giue, which 19. minutes are the diuersitie of the 9. and 10. degrées of Taurus. So I finde that 14. minutes giueth 17. minutes, and 6. seconds, which 17. minutes and 6. seconds, I adde to the 14. degrées. 23. minutes, which answereth to the 9 degrées of Taurus. And it commeth to 14. degrées 49. minutes, and 6. seconds, which is the true declination of the 20. day of Aprill, Anno. 1561.

It is also to be noted, that I adde these 17. minutes and 6. secondes, because the declination dooth increase: for if it decreased, it were to bee taken out so much, and the rest is the declination. So is the declination for the twentie of Aprill, in the yeare 1561. fourtéene degrées, 49. minutes, and sixe seconds.

FINIS

AT LONDON.
Printed by Edward Allde, and
are to bee ſolde by Hugh Aſtley,
dwelling at Saint Magnus corner.
Anno. 1596.

www.ingramcontent.com/pod-product-compliance
Lightning Source LLC
Chambersburg PA
CBHW020035030726
47499CB00007B/2428
9783337127596